CW00540164

Cover design by Jan Sigetty Boeje
https://www.facebook.com/pages/Sigettys Cover Design

Special thanks to my editors Jean Pacillo
http://www.ebookeditingpro.com

and Janell Parque
http://janellparque.blogspot.com

———

To be the first to hear about new releases and bargains from Willow Rose, sign up below to be on the VIP List. (I promise not to share your email with anyone else, and I won't clutter your inbox.)

- TAP HERE TO SIGN UP TO BE ON THE VIP LIST -

Tired of too many emails? Text the word: "willowrose" to 31996 to sign up to Willow's VIP text List to get a text alert with news about New Releases, Giveaways, Bargains and Free books from Willow.

FOLLOW WILLOW ROSE ON BOOKBUB:

Follow Willow on BookBub

Connect with Willow online:
Facebook
Twitter
GoodReads
willow-rose.net
madamewillowrose@gmail.com

EMMA FROST MYSTERY - BOOK 1

ITSY BITSY SPIDER

WILLOW ROSE

BOOKS BY THE AUTHOR

HARRY HUNTER MYSTERY SERIES

- ALL THE GOOD GIRLS
- RUN GIRL RUN
- NO OTHER WAY
- NEVER WALK ALONE

MARY MILLS MYSTERY SERIES

- WHAT HURTS THE MOST
- YOU CAN RUN
- YOU CAN'T HIDE
- CAREFUL LITTLE EYES

EVA RAE THOMAS MYSTERY SERIES

- DON'T LIE TO ME
- WHAT YOU DID
- NEVER EVER
- SAY YOU LOVE ME
- LET ME GO
- IT'S NOT OVER
- NOT DEAD YET
- TO DIE FOR

EMMA FROST SERIES

- ITSY BITSY SPIDER
- MISS DOLLY HAD A DOLLY

- Run, Run as Fast as You Can
- Cross Your Heart and Hope to Die
- Peek-a-Boo I See You
- Tweedledum and Tweedledee
- Easy as One, Two, Three
- There's No Place like Home
- Slenderman
- Where the Wild Roses Grow
- Waltzing Mathilda
- Drip Drop Dead
- Black Frost

JACK RYDER SERIES

- Hit the Road Jack
- Slip out the Back Jack
- The House that Jack Built
- Black Jack
- Girl Next Door
- Her Final Word
- Don't Tell

REBEKKA FRANCK SERIES

- One, Two...He is Coming for You
- Three, Four...Better Lock Your Door
- Five, Six...Grab your Crucifix
- Seven, Eight...Gonna Stay up Late
- Nine, Ten...Never Sleep Again
- Eleven, Twelve...Dig and Delve
- Thirteen, Fourteen...Little Boy Unseen
- Better Not Cry
- Ten Little Girls
- It Ends Here

MYSTERY/THRILLER/HORROR NOVELS

- In One Fell Swoop
- Umbrella Man
- Blackbird Fly
- To Hell in a Handbasket
- Edwina

HORROR SHORT-STORIES

- Mommy Dearest
- The Bird
- Better watch out
- Eenie, Meenie
- Rock-a-Bye Baby
- Nibble, Nibble, Crunch
- Humpty Dumpty
- Chain Letter

PARANORMAL SUSPENSE/ROMANCE NOVELS

- In Cold Blood
- The Surge
- Girl Divided

THE VAMPIRES OF SHADOW HILLS SERIES

- Flesh and Blood

- Blood and Fire
- Fire and Beauty
- Beauty and Beasts
- Beasts and Magic
- Magic and Witchcraft
- Witchcraft and War
- War and Order
- Order and Chaos
- Chaos and Courage

THE AFTERLIFE SERIES

- Beyond
- Serenity
- Endurance
- Courageous

THE WOLFBOY CHRONICLES

- A Gypsy Song
- I am WOLF

DAUGHTERS OF THE JAGUAR

- Savage
- Broken

The Itsy Bitsy Spider crawled up the waterspout.
Down came the rain, and washed the spider out.
Out came the sun, and dried up all the rain,
And the Itsy Bitsy Spider went up the spout again.

NURSERY RHYME

PROLOGUE
1977

At first she thought it was an accident that the door to the bunker had shut. Then she tried to open it on her own, but couldn't. It was either too heavy or it must have locked when it shut. She knocked carefully.

"Hello?"

The quiet coming from outside the iron door was almost cruel. Astrid swallowed and knocked once again, this time harder.

"Hello?"

But nothing. Nothing but the horrendous sound of her own breathing. *Someone will open it. Once they realize it has shut, they'll come.* Astrid took the few steps from the door down into the bunker. She felt tired and her feet were swollen. She sighed and sat down on a bench, waiting, staring at the door, and anticipating it swinging open at any moment now. Except, it was actually two doors, separated by a small hallway between them. So even if she hammered, they wouldn't be able to hear her. All she could do was wait. Someone would eventually come for her.

Wouldn't they? Of course they would. He would come. He who told her he loved her...

Astrid knew she wasn't among the smartest of the young kids on the island. Her mother always told her that. But Astrid had good hands and she wasn't a half-bad cook. If she stuck to what she knew, she might be lucky enough to one day have a man, her mother had promised. Now Astrid had found one. And he wanted more than just her cooking. He wanted her. He loved her, he said. Then he made love to her in the dunes by the beach.

He was nice to her and she wanted him to meet her mother, but he kept telling her: *not now, not today.* Astrid never thought of asking when. She just waited patiently for him to find the time in his busy schedule. She never wondered why he never took her places, or why he insisted they only meet at night, or why he never spoke to her except for the dirty words he whispered in her ears; Astrid was educated enough to know that these words weren't something they would say in church.

No, Astrid never thought there could be anything wrong with her relationship with this boy who once said he loved her, and who showed his love for her in the dunes again and again, night after night, during that endless summer in 1977. Instead, she started looking forward to their life together, preparing herself to one day become his wife, and to have a baby.

"You'll get nothing but dummies like yourself," her mother had said. "There should be a law that demanded that people like you were sterilized so you wouldn't pass your stupidity on to your kids. Stupid girl," she said, and slapped Astrid across the face.

Yes, Astrid was very well aware that she wasn't the smartest among people, but she had a good heart. That much she knew. One day she would become a great mother to a child who would have its father's intellect, and that child was going to go out into the world and do great things.

"That'll show them," she said, sniffling, while staring at the closed iron door at the top of the stairs.

"He'll come for me, won't he?" she asked, and her voice echoed into the small room behind her that was lit only by a lightbulb hanging from under the ceiling. *Of course he will. Of course.*

Astrid drew in a deep sigh. She looked around and spotted the big flashlight on a shelf in the corner among blankets, water bottles, and canned food. She pulled the flashlight out and held it in her hand. Then she sat down again, waiting for someone to come and get her. *Not just someone. Him, the boy of her dreams, the love of her life. Not just anyone.*

Astrid sighed and calmed herself down. She always did this, her mother would say; she always made herself uneasy or even anxious for no reason at all.

1

2012

The man was looking in the windows of the French doors leading into the kitchen. It was dark inside the mansion by the ocean. A small light under the door revealed that there was someone in the other room next to the kitchen. Just as he had hoped.

The man lifted his gloved hand and smashed it through the small window, then reached through and unlocked the door. He opened it without making any sound at all. Smoothly, he slid through the door and into the woman's kitchen. Carefully, he closed the door behind him, while stepping on the broken glass strewn underneath his heavy boots.

The man turned and looked at the perfect kitchen. Knives were hanging on the wall. He grabbed one and looked at it in the moonlight that poured into the room. Then he sighed with a deep feeling of satisfaction while putting it back. He reached into his own sports bag and found his own set of knives rolled up in their bag. Like a professional chef, he unfolded the bag and rolled the knives out on the table.

What a beautiful sight to his eyes. Clean blades, sharpened to perfection. Almost a pity he had to mess them up. Cutting through meat and bones always made them dull. The man picked one out and put the rest back in his bag. Then he approached the door leading to the adjacent room, where he could tell the TV was on.

The man had studied the woman's daily routine for weeks now and knew she always dozed off to her favorite show, *The Sopranos*, before she awoke and went to the bathroom at exactly ten-thirty. She was as precise as a clock. Then she would go into the kitchen and grab a glass of water to put next to her bed for the night. She seemed to have a hard time sleeping lately and he speculated that this made her thirsty.

The man walked out of the kitchen door and into the hallway as he heard the theme song for *The Sopranos*, and then the TV went silent.

The man sat down on a chair in the corner of the guest bedroom and waited, listening to the woman performing her routines, like he had done many times before, but this time was different. This was the big finish, *le grand finale*, as they said in French.

The man glanced at his reflection in the mirror on the dresser. He touched his pale skin and followed one of the veins with his finger. Then he smiled at himself. He had been looking forward to this moment for all of his life. He had prepared for it, dreamt about it, arranged it into details, just waiting for the right time and to be in the right place.

And the best of it? He was just starting out.

2

2012

Old Mrs. Heinrichsen let out a small shriek. The spider in her bathroom sink had startled her. They always did. She shook her head and turned on the tap. The spider tried to fight the river of water, clinging on to the slippery side as the water was threatening to flush it down the drain. Mrs. Heinrichsen watched its struggle with great joy and turned the tap to speed up the water. She grinned and sang while watching the spider fight for its life.

"The Itsy Bitsy Spider crawled up the water spout.
Down came the rain, and washed the spider out.
Out came the sun, and dried up all the rain,
And the Itsy Bitsy Spider went up the spout again."

Finally, the spider gave up, lost the fight, and disappeared with the water into the drain. The old woman liked these small displays of power over nature. She had always enjoyed them over humans as well, but in recent years, respect for her and her status on the small island had diminished. No one seemed to care who she was or who she had been anymore.

There was a time when it wasn't only spiders that had struggled to stay alive by her mercy. Oh, how she missed those days. How she missed seeing the fear and terror in people's eyes as she drove down the street in her new car, or went for a stroll showing off her newest fur brought in from Paris, or a new jumpsuit from Milan. Those were the days. Those were the times she had cherished and would remember as her golden years.

But these days, no one cared anymore. No one respected her in the manner they had back then. To them, she was just an old lady. Someone whose time was ticking down. Someone who was close to the finish line of life. The youngsters of today didn't have any respect for status or title anymore. It was all just the same baloney to them. They didn't care about her position; hell, most of them hardly knew her name anymore.

Mrs. Heinrichsen finished brushing her teeth and walked back towards the bedroom. The old wooden floors of her villa creaked underneath her weight, even though she could hardly make it past ninety pounds anymore. She was still a strong woman and she expected to live at least twenty years more.

"Gotta make it past the one hundred mark," she always said. "Get the letter from the queen before you go."

It was her goal, and Mrs. Heinrichsen always reached her goals. This was something she had tried to teach her son, but in vain. Today, people didn't seem to care about setting goals and reaching them, or about doing what it took to make it, no matter what the cost. Working to accomplish something. Nowadays it was all about how to get out of working and how to get the state to pay for everything. She saw people like this down by the harbor, down by the boats leading to the mainland. These people who could just as well be working, but here they were instead, drinking their beers, hanging out with their dogs, and sporting dirty clothes. Mrs. Heinrichsen knew they got paid from the state to live that kind of life. Destitute was the nice word for them. People who couldn't take care of themselves, so the state had to step in. Freeloaders, Mrs. Heinrichsen would call them. In her book, they were nothing but people who didn't want to work. And lately, with all those newcomers, all those brown people who had almost invaded the country, even their small island, and were all being paid huge amounts from the state to get all their relatives up here, it was about to destroy the small paradise, destroy Denmark with all their demands, under the pretense that they just wanted to be *equal*. How those dirty faces could ever get the thought that they were equal to the proud hardworking Danish people, she never understood. It was an atrocity. The beautiful country had been invaded by these...these foreigners...and Mrs. Heinrichsen certainly didn't like what they were turning this country into.

Mrs. Heinrichsen entered her bedroom and sat on her bed wearily. It had become increasingly difficult for her to lie down with her breathing troubles, and she wasn't looking forward to yet another night sitting up and sleeping. The nights had become long and painful to her lately and even though she did take a small nightcap, it never quite helped her through the entire night.

"Oh, John. You bastard," she said, and looked at the empty side of the bed where he used to sleep. "I bet you're up there somewhere enjoying seeing me suffer through these nights, aren't you?"

The silence from the room was answer enough. Mrs. Heinrichsen leaned back on her stack of pillows and hugged her arms around her body. Barely had she closed her eyes before she heard a sound. Mrs. Heinrichsen got out of the bed again with much discomfort.

"If it's that neighbor's dog again, I'm sure I'm gonna..."

She never made it further than that. As she fought to get out of the bed and up onto her feet, she watched the door to her bedroom open quietly. Then she gasped.

A face appeared in the darkness.

"Hello, Agnes," the man said.

3

2012

"I can't believe you inherited a real house, Mommy."

I looked through the rearview mirror at my seven-year-old son, Victor, sitting in the back seat of our old Toyota. He was smiling and his small eyes sparkled. He had been so excited ever since we received the phone call telling me that my grandmother, my father's mother, had passed away, and much to my surprise, since I never knew her, that she had left her house to me.

My oldest child, my daughter Maya, was less excited, to put it mildly. But then again, at thirteen, not much was exciting, especially if it involved me, her mother, or anything remotely grown up and boring.

"Of course she inherited it, you doofus," Maya said to her younger brother. "She's her only grandchild."

"Well she could have left it to grandpa, her son," I argued, while finding my exit from the highway. "That would have been the most normal thing to do. But for some reason, she wanted me to have it."

"Why?" Maya asked with her lips curled, making her look like she was extremely annoyed.

I shrugged. "I don't know. I never even knew her. Grandpa says I met her once when I was just a small child, but I don't remember it. Maybe I chose to forget because she was too scary," I said, and made a funny face.

Maya looked mad. "You're so...so pathetic."

"Wow. Well, thanks."

That seemed to be the end of that conversation. It had been a long ride from Copenhagen to Esbjerg, and my children hadn't exactly been talking much. It was getting dark outside the car's windows and would be way past their bedtime by the time we arrived at our new house.

Victor had slept most of the way and Maya seemed to feel it was beneath her dignity to talk to me for more than three minutes at a time. She was pissed because I had made the decision for all of us. I had decided to move there, to my grandmother's house on Fanoe, a small island in the North Sea outside of Esbjerg. I knew it wouldn't be popular to make a decision like that on my children's behalf, but there was no way around it. I was broke and couldn't afford to keep our apartment in Copenhagen. I had been fired from my latest job as a writer for a fishing magazine, simply because I had pissed off the chairman of the Danish Fishing Federation, DFF, by asking him about the many bottles of expensive wine that the Federation had deducted on their taxes this year. Needless to say, it wasn't the kind of story that the magazine was looking for, so they kicked me out. Well, that's just the way things go. I wasn't exactly looking for a long-term career in fishing journalism anyway, but it had been a paying job, and it had allowed me to bring home enough money for the rent and expenses that my ex had left me with when he decided it was more fun to be with a twenty-five-year old intern at his TV station than to stay with his family.

"Are we there soon?" Victor asked with a slight whimper.

"Why?" I asked. "You need to go?"

Victor nodded heavily. "Badly."

Maya sighed and rolled her eyes. "You could have gone when we stopped for snacks."

"I did," Victor said.

"But that's only, like, ten minutes ago. How can you need to go already? We've stopped twenty times for you on this trip." Maya shot him an annoyed look.

"Maya. Your brother..."

"Has a nervous bladder. I know. There's always something with him, isn't there?"

That shut me up for once. What was I supposed to say? Yes, there is always something wrong with your brother? Yes, he suffers from anxiety attacks, light autism, strange seizures, occasional loss of bladder control, and maybe some other stuff that the doctors are just waiting to throw at us? Yes, he hasn't been well ever since his dad just took off and only wanted to see him every six months or whenever it suited him? Yes, I could say all those things, but I didn't. What's the point anyway? She knew. Maya knew Victor hadn't been well and she was suffering too, suffering because every hour of my attention went towards him. She was a big girl, now. She was supposed to be able to handle it.

"What's that smell?" she asked, and wrinkled her nose.

"That, my friend, is the smell of Esbjerg," I said and smiled, as I could see the town rise in front of us. "We'll take the boat out to the island from there. It'll be fun once we're on the boat. Just wait and see."

"Yay!" Victor exclaimed. "I love boats."

"It smells like fish," Maya said, and held her nose.

I had to admit, the smell was pretty bad, and opening the window only made it worse. "It's fish," I said, trying to sound cheerful. "Fish guts."

4

1977

It didn't take Astrid many hours to lose track of time, but she guessed it was getting closer to nighttime, since she was beginning to become tired. She decided to lay down a little bit and closed her eyes, and soon she was sound asleep.

It wasn't until the morning that the panic erupted inside of her. She woke up and realized she was still trapped in the bunker and now she was beginning to feel hungry. She got up and walked to the door again. Then she started hammering it.

"Help!" she yelled, but then felt bad. Her mother always told her not to raise her voice.

"You're always so loud, Astrid. And shrill. You should learn to keep your mouth shut. You don't have a pretty voice, and boys like pretty voices, so you stick to what you can do. You cook, alright?"

"Yes, Mom."

Astrid took a deep breath and decided to try again, even if she didn't like to be loud. "HEEELP! I'm in here! I'm trapped! Christian? Can you hear me?"

She stopped and listened for footsteps, or maybe even voices. But still there was nothing. Nothing but the terror of silence.

She tried again. This time she clenched her fists and hammered with all her strength against the iron door, and continued till the pads of her hands became numb. Then she managed to put her fingers into the small crack and tried to rip the door open, but it was stuck.

"Help!" she yelled, while the feeling of utter panic grew.

What if no one hears me? No, you stupid fool. Don't think like that.

She tried to scratch the door with her fingernails, but had to stop because it hurt. Astrid sat down on the step and covered her face with her hands. She was so hungry now. She looked up at the ceiling.

Maybe there was another way out? There had to be an air vent somewhere. Astrid got up and went to the end wall with the shelves. She removed some blankets and touched the wall behind it, felt it, scanned it for anything that could indicate that there was some secret passageway or even a small hole that she could get through.

But there was nothing. She went through the stuff on the shelves meticulously, in the hope that she could find something to use to break the door open. But there was nothing but the flashlight. She rose with it in her hand and ran towards the iron door, swinging and smashing it against the door, but it didn't even make a bump.

She cried as she swung it again and again and destroyed the plastic casing, but it never harmed the door in any way.

Astrid fell to the cold stairs.

You really are no good, are you? She heard her mother's voice say. *Got yourself into trouble again. I knew you would. He's not going to take care of you. Be a damned fool if he did.*

No, no, Dr. Jansen says I'm okay, remember? I'm good and healthy and strong. My man doesn't care about me being smart or anything. He loves me, he said.

You fool. No one loves a retard. No one, I tell you. No one!

Astrid wiped off her tears in disgust. Why did thinking of her mother always do that to her? Why did it always make her feel so bad about herself? No, there had to be a way, there had to be. Astrid stared at the canned food on the shelves, then sprang up and pulled one down. Luckily it was one of those you could pull open. She didn't even need a can opener. This was good, she thought to herself as she pulled the tab and the sweet smell of ravioli hit her nostrils and tricked her deep hunger even more. This was very good. Astrid searched everywhere and finally found a bunch of plastic spoons. Relieved, she sat down and started eating.

Things always looked better on a full stomach, mother used to say. So as soon as Astrid finished this can, she would find a way to get out of there.

5

―――――

2012

We took the last ferry to get to the island. I had to stop at the local police station to pick up the key to the house as soon as we arrived. It was almost midnight when we finally found the right place. Everything was dark and the wind had picked up in the almost barren trees outside. I walked through a pile of dead leaves someone must have raked earlier before I entered the small building that was apparently called a police station. The kids wanted to stay in the car. Victor was asleep and Maya was listening to music on her iPhone. I was tired and looking very much forward to finally entering my future home and throwing myself on one of the beds. The house was still furnished, I had been told by the lawyer who gave me the deed to the house. I took that as a sign that I could move in right away.

"Are you serious?" Maya had exclaimed when I had told her back at the apartment. "Do you really want to live in some dead woman's old furniture?"

"We'll get our own shipped over there eventually, but until then, yes. Plus, it's a really big house. We don't have enough furniture to fill it up. I bet my grandmother's was nice. She was loaded, you know."

"Couldn't she just have left us the money instead?" my smart daughter had argued. "Then we could build our own house or stay in our own apartment and not have to leave the city for some deserted island where only freaks would live."

"She left her money to your grandpa, who's the rightful heir to it, being her son. I was just...I'm sorry...*we* were just lucky that we got this splendid house out of it. I didn't expect to get anything."

"How do you know it was luck? Maybe the house is really her way of getting back at you," Maya had said before going to her room.

I stuck my tongue out after her, and then had returned to my packing.

The police station looked deserted when I entered. There was no one behind the counter.

"Excuse me?" I said and cleared my throat. "Hello?"

"Freeze!" a voice said next to me.

I gasped and jumped. A guy in uniform came out of a door, pointing his fingers at me to make them look like a gun. I raised both arms. He laughed.

"Boy, you scared me," I said, and looked at him the way my annoying teenager did at me.

The police officer laughed. I hadn't noticed until then, but he was quite handsome. Blond with blue eyes, tall and very masculine. About my age, maybe a little older, but it was hard to tell. "I'm sorry," he said. "I don't get out much, as you can imagine. I don't get to have much fun either. Especially not at night. Boy, you should have seen the look on your face."

"That was not funny. My heart is still racing."

The man grinned. "I'm sorry," he said again. "I really didn't mean to. It was just so tempting."

"Okay, okay. I get it," I said. "Maybe there's a reason they don't let you get out much, huh? Maybe they keep you on the nightshift for a reason?"

The officer tilted his head. "I never thought about it that way. Hmm. Maybe you're right."

"You bet I am."

"I'm Officer Dan," he said, and reached out his hand. "Dan Toft."

I smiled and took it. "Emma Frost."

"Nice to meet you, Emma Frost," he said, and kept shaking my hand.

"Likewise, Officer Dan."

He let go of my hand and went behind the counter. "What can I do for you at this strange hour? Are you visiting our island?"

"No. We're actually moving here. I was supposed to pick up the key here? At least that's what my lawyer told me. I thought it sounded strange but..."

I never finished the sentence before Officer Dan dangled the keys in front of my face. "These should be the ones. We do all kinds of jobs for the public here in this station. Yesterday, I walked Mrs. Olson's puppy, since she had fallen and hurt her leg and couldn't walk it herself. Keeping people's house keys is the least of our jobs. It's kind of nice, though. We get to know people closely that way."

"Plus, it means you don't have much else to do, right? You must not have much crime here on the island. Must be kind of nice, right?" I said and took the keys out of his hand.

"It sure is," he responded.

"Well, thanks," I said and started walking towards the door.

Officer Dan ran in front of me and held it open for me. I chuckled.

"See you around," he said as I walked out.

I caught myself thinking I would really like that.

6

2012

He was wondering what kind of mood the old hag was in today as he waited for the garage door to open so he could pull into the driveway. The gravel crunched loudly underneath the wheels of the Mercedes. Why she insisted on still driving this old car when she could easily afford a newer model, Torben didn't understand. But it was her car and her money.

Torben had worked for Mrs. Heinrichsen for as long as he could remember. Drove her around wherever she needed to go. Did some handiwork around the house whenever it was needed, or at least made sure the right people were called to fix it. He was her *go-to guy,* as they said in the movies. Torben didn't mind that. In fact, he enjoyed being needed by someone. Ever since his wife had passed away six years ago, the old house seemed so empty. The kids had moved away many years ago, off to the mainland, to the big city to lives of their own and they soon forgot all about their old father rotting away on the island.

Back in the day when Mr. Heinrichsen was still alive, Torben had not liked his job very much. He simply didn't like Mr. Heinrichsen and the way he treated people. Well, the old lady wasn't much better herself, and age didn't seem to soften her up, but Torben had known her for many years now and knew she wasn't so bad once you really got to know her. She would boss him around, yes, but now that Yvonne wasn't alive anymore, he quite frankly liked to have someone tell him what to do from time to time. It had that familiar feeling to it. Like he had a purpose.

Torben broke out of his reverie and fixed his cap and tie to make sure they were on straight. Mrs. Heinrichsen preferred him to look right. She didn't like sloppiness, and over the years, Torben had learned to appreciate this fact. You didn't find much of that these days anymore. Discipline, self-control. It was all in the character, and Mrs. Heinrichsen had helped Torben build his character. She had made him stronger. Not with a loving and caring attitude, but by being harsh and hard on him when he needed it the most. Like when Yvonne died. It had nearly broken him. He was about to slide into a deep depression, when Mrs. Heinrichsen told him to stop feeling sorry for himself.

"Just get over it," she had said.

She had given him a day off to go to the funeral, actually a whole week, but the next day he had shown up at her doorstep, his cap in his hand, asking her if she needed him today. He could tell by the look in her eyes that she hadn't any plans, but she had come up with some.

"As a matter of fact, you're late," she had said, with her well-known snort that Torben had hated so much, but suddenly found very comforting, very familiar. "I have to see my hairdresser in ten minutes and with all this traffic, it's going to take at least fifteen."

"Then let's get going," he said with a huge smile, and brought the car out. Of course the old lady didn't have an appointment, but the hairdressers found time for her anyway. She had a way like that. She could make people jump for her.

That was when Torben realized the old woman did have a heart.

They never talked about the death of Yvonne or Torben's sadness again, but they didn't have to. Somehow, they had found each other, a strange sort of friendship in the middle of it all, and that was enough for him. He didn't need her pity or her compassion. He needed everything to go back to normal, and so it had. It made coming home to the empty house a lot easier when he knew there was someone needing him in the morning.

Torben whistled and waited in the driveway for the big old wooden door to open, but minutes passed and nothing happened. Torben wrinkled his nose. In all the thirty years Torben had worked for the lady, she had never ever been late once. A feeling of unease was starting to spread in his body as the minutes passed by, and finally, he couldn't stand it anymore. Mrs. Heinrichsen was supposed to be at her lawyer's office on the mainland at ten, and if she didn't come out now, they weren't going to catch the ferry.

Torben knew Mrs. Heinrichsen would be very angry with him for doing this, but something compelled him to walk up the stairs and walk into the big old house.

"Hello?" he said, hoping Mrs. Heinrichsen had merely overslept. "Mrs. Heinrichsen? The car is ready for you? The ferry leaves in half an hour."

As he received no answer, Torben's heart started racing in his chest. This was not good, he thought, and ran up the stairs and down the hallway. He knocked on her bedroom door with his cap in his hand.

"Mrs. Heinrichsen. We're going to be late."

He knocked twice, three times, and when there was still no answer, he took in a deep breath and did what he had never done before. He walked into Mrs. Heinrichsen's bedroom.

"I'm sorry to do this but..."

Torben froze at the sight of the old lady lying on her bed with her empty eyes staring into the ceiling. Then he cried. Not because he was reminded of the time he had come home and found his wife in the same position, dead from a heart attack on the same bed where she had given birth to their two sons, and not because he was sad that he was now going to be really alone, since no one would need his services any longer. No, Torben cried because of what had happened to Mrs. Heinrichsen's body. He cried and sobbed because never in his sixty years of living had he been in the presence of such cruelty.

7

___

2012

I was woken by the sound of sirens in the street. My sleep had been uneasy and it had been very late before I even got to put my head on the pillow. I glanced at my phone.

"For God's sake. It's eight am. I might as well be back in the city with all that noise."

I looked out the window and saw the island's police car (yes I would later learn that there was actually only one!) drive past my new house. It stopped further down the street in front of what looked like a big gate. I rubbed my eyes and decided to take a shower. I had a busy day ahead of me, unpacking our boxes and getting to know our new home.

Only a few minutes later, Victor was jumping around downstairs. I had barely managed to find the pots and pans to begin making the bacon and eggs I had brought with us in a cooler.

"This house is awesome!" he exclaimed.

I couldn't help smiling. It had been a long time since I had seen him this happy. It warmed my heart and filled me with hope for our future.

"Are you hungry, buddy? I'm making eggs and toast and..."

"Mom, have you even seen the yard yet?" he asked, his eyes sparkling.

"No I have not had the pleasure..."

Victor jumped up and pulled my arm. "You won't believe it. It has Douglas firs, it has ash, and birches, and even cypresses."

"Oh, really, huh?" I said sleepily, while my son dragged me through the beautiful old living room and through the doors leading to the backyard. To me, it looked mostly like a wild forest, but I knew to Victor it was like heaven. He had been into trees for several years now and always complained that living in the city was dull and dead, *we might as well live on the space station circling the earth*, he would say. He loved trees and always dreamed of having his own yard. I smiled and put my arm around him, forgetting how he hated to be touched. For a second, he forgot as well. While he watched the big dark trees that were completely blocking the view of the ocean beneath the yard, I got to hold on to him for just a few seconds, something I hadn't been able to do in years without him breaking into a hysterical scream.

Then he remembered and pushed away my arm. He walked closer and looked up at the mighty trees in front of him.

I pushed back a tear, watching him. He looked like he was dancing between them, turning on his feet, almost glowing. "Don't get lost in there," I said, half laughing, half choking. "I'll get that breakfast ready for you in a jiff," I added, and walked back towards the kitchen.

I chuckled with happiness as I put bread in the toaster and found out how to work the stove.

"What's all the fuss about?" Maya had just walked into the kitchen and was looking at me like I was a babbling idiot.

"Victor is excited about the trees in the yard. Have you seen all the big trees? You know how much he has always wanted to live in a house with a yard full of trees."

"That's so..." Maya stopped herself from saying something. I guessed she could tell by the look in my eyes that this was not the moment for one of her usual sarcastic remarks.

I smiled and served the breakfast. I called for Victor and he came storming inside with the biggest smile on his face.

"Don't stuff your mouth," I said, but didn't mean it. I was glad to see him eat like a healthy happy boy and not simply pick at his food with a fork, claiming that he wasn't hungry as usual. This was certainly the change he needed; if not for anyone else, then it was certainly good for him, and that was enough for me.

"So, what, are there, like, schools here?" Maya asked, carefully avoiding the bacon and sticking to the egg and toast.

"Of course I've already contacted them and they know you're coming. Starting next week after we've settled in. You have four days off till then."

Maya scoffed. Victor didn't seem to notice anything. He swallowed the rest of his food and left the table.

"Don't forget your plate." But it was too late. I ate the rest of his bacon and then took some more from the pan.

"You know that stuff is really bad for you, don't you?" Maya said.

"I do. But I also know that I like food and I like to eat and I'm not a teenager anymore, so I don't have to worry about my appearance constantly." I took another piece and crunched it between my teeth, just to be defiant.

"I thought you wanted to lose weight. It's all you talked about when we were back at the apartment. How you thought moving to a new place might help you get back into shape and so on."

I grimaced. "Well, sue me for being happy. I'll start running again. I used to love running."

"Yeah, right, that'll happen."

"Really? Is that what we're doing now? Making fun of me because I'm a little on the chubby side, is it? Seriously, Maya. Can't you just lay off the witty remarks for once and try to enjoy this new adventure?"

Maya snorted, and then she got up from her chair. "Well, it's an adventure for you maybe. And for that tree hugger out there, the little weirdo, but what about me?"

"What about you, Maya?" I asked, annoyed. "Not everything is about you, you know?"

"Nothing is ever about me!" she yelled.

I was startled by the tone in her voice. It sounded so much like when she was younger, back when she still needed her mother to fix everything. It dawned on me that maybe she still did need me after all, that maybe she wasn't as grown up as she had pretended to be.

"What are you saying, Maya?"

"I'm saying that you just made this decision to move all of us here without even asking me. It's all about what you want, what you need, or what Victor needs. It's never about what I want. I had friends. I had good friends. I might never see them again. How do you think that feels?"

"Maya. Sweetie. Of course you'll see them again. You'll go on holidays and maybe some weekends. We'll figure it out."

"And what about Dad?"

I sighed. "What about him?"

"Will we ever get to see him again, or have you just decided that he's out of our lives as well?"

"That is not my decision to make, Maya, and you know it. Your father was the one who moved out. He was the one who said his girlfriend couldn't handle you. Not me. I wanted you to see him; I wanted you to go there every other weekend like most kids in a divorce, but he made the choice. He made the decision, Maya. Not me."

"Because of Victor," she cried. "Because they couldn't handle Victor and all his seizures and panic attacks. That's why. Not because of me."

I exhaled deeply. "Maya, sweetie..." I paused. Her eyes told me she couldn't handle the truth yet. The fact was that her father had said he couldn't handle either of them, that his girlfriend couldn't stand them, and it was too much for her now that she was pregnant and all. That was the truth. But at this moment I realized it would break Maya's heart if I told her that, so instead I kept quiet. This was not the time for that.

"Maya...I..."

"See, I told you. I'm just not important enough. You made that decision because of Victor, right? Just like you made the decision to move here based on what was best for Victor. Not me. Never me."

Maya ran out the door and slammed it behind her. I looked down at my plate and finished the rest of the bacon, feeling all kinds of guilt.

"I'll start running tomorrow," I mumbled, and drank the rest of my juice.

8

2012

I decided to put our fight behind me and started unpacking the boxes I had managed to carry in last night. As soon as I was done with those, I walked back to the car to get the rest. I opened the back and carried them out one by one, when I suddenly stopped. The police car was still parked in the street further down the road, and now the entrance had been blocked off with police tape. But that wasn't what struck me, even though four hours or so had passed by. No, what caught my attention were the two blue vans parked inside the police blockade, next to the island's only police car.

Those weren't just ordinary vans; I knew that from my time as a real reporter on one of the local papers in Copenhagen. These were the vans from the Forensic team. These guys were only called out if it was a murder case.

My curiosity got the better of me and I put down the box I was holding and walked closer. I joined the small crowd of neighbors and passersby who had stopped to watch. Behind the tape I spotted several people in blue bodysuits searching the place, picking up small pieces of evidence with tweezers and securing them in plastic bags.

"I-I-Interesting, huh?" a man standing next to me asked.

"Excuse me?" I asked and looked at him. My first thought was that he was some kind of weirdo, with his brown beanie covering his hair and forehead, and those black clothes and his stooping posture. He had both of his hands in his pockets like he was cold, but it was warm outside. But something in his eyes made me think twice. They seemed nice.

"W-w-what h-h-happened?" he said.

I shrugged. "I don't know. I just got here."

"Y-y-you're...t-t-that...n-n-new o-o-one, right?" he stuttered horribly, and I think the fact that I was now looking at him made it even worse.

I smiled compassionately and nodded, knowing how fast news spread in a small place like this. "Yes. We just moved in."

"W-w-welcome...I'm...J-j-jack. I...I...l-l-live a-a-across f-f-from y-y-you."

"Well, hi then, Jack," I said, and for some strange reason couldn't help thinking about Jack the Ripper. Jack wasn't a common Danish name, but I didn't want to ask him about it, since I knew that would require him to speak more than one sentence. I had never known anyone who stuttered before and was afraid to somehow embarrass him.

"It's just because he doesn't know you yet," a woman standing to my other side said.

I turned and looked at her. She seemed to be about my age, the beginning or middle of her thirties, maybe a little more. "Sorry?"

"Jack always stutters when he gets nervous. New people make him nervous. Especially when they're pretty like you."

I almost laughed, but I could tell she was serious.

"Hi, I'm Sophia. I live next to Jack on the other side of the street across from your house. The cheap side." She reached out her hand and I took it.

"Emma," I said.

"Got any kids, Emma?" Sophia asked.

"Two. A teenage daughter and a seven-year-old son."

Sophia nodded. "Good for you. I have five. All with different fathers. I'll tell you about them one day, but you'll have to bring the wine."

I chuckled. "I will. Do you have any idea what happened here?"

"Old Mrs. Heinrichsen was found dead this morning. That's all I know so far. Not that she'll be missed around here, old hag."

"Oh," I said, and looked at the scene. I spotted Officer Dan among the people in there. He saw me, too, and waved.

"So, what do you do, Emma?" Sophia asked. "For a living."

"Well, I'm a writer."

"Written anything interesting lately?" she asked.

"Nope. Still waiting for that million-dollar idea for the bestseller I'm planning on living off of for the rest of my life. Until then, I'm living off the money I got from selling my apartment in Copenhagen."

"Should keep you going for a long time out here," Sophia said. "Not much to spend money on unless you like to buy tourist crap."

"I really don't," I said. "Well, better get back to the kids."

"Shoot! The kids!" Sophia said and walked back with me. "Keep forgetting about them. Must be wishful thinking, huh? See you around," she added and waved as she walked away.

I waved back, thinking it was going to be easy to make friends here.

It was in the moment that I turned and looked back at the scene that it struck me.

I should write about this. I should write a book about the murder on Fanoe Island.

9

1977

There was a small toilet and a sink in the corner of the room that Astrid used to throw up in in the mornings. The nausea had grown worse, and so did her worry that no one was going to come after her...that they had somehow forgotten about her.

Or maybe they were, in fact, looking for her; maybe *he* was looking for her up there, but was looking in all the wrong places?

But you don't believe that anymore, do you?

It was hot in the bunker and Astrid was happy that she had worn a dress on the day that she had been trapped down there. It was expandable and too big, so there was room to grow.

Days went by—at least she felt like it was days—it might have been weeks without a sound from the outside. From time to time, Astrid hammered her fists on the iron door and yelled and screamed at the top of her lungs, but soon she gave up the fight. It was useless. It was a horrifying thought, cruel and gruesome beyond anything, but she was beginning to think that maybe, just maybe, she was stuck down here forever, or at least until the rations of food and water ran out. Then she would surely starve to death eventually. The thought made her start to cry again, but there were no more tears left. She

fought hard not to allow the thoughts of a slow death caused by starvation and thirst enter her fragile mind and poison her spirit, but it
was a fight she knew she would lose. Was death really the only way
out of this shithole?

"Won't anyone miss me?" she mumbled and heard the echo of her
own voice. "Mom? Christian? Anyone?"

Are you even looking for me?

The feeling of loneliness crept up on her and she hugged her
blanket just not to feel so alone. For a long time—only God knows
how long—she sat staring at the barren walls and the packed shelves
with food enough for what? A month? Two? At least enough for now.

*You mustn't give up. Don't give up the fight. Don't give in to those
bitter thoughts. You're not a failure till you've given up the fight.*

Astrid sniffled and wiped her nose with the back of her hand.
This was not the time to throw a pity-party, she convinced herself.
Sad thoughts like these would only drag her down, only make things
worse. Since there wasn't anything she could do to change her situation, Astrid decided to make the best of what she had. So, to keep the
boredom away, she started stacking cans in high towers. She had
made five that reached all the way to the ceiling and only needed one
more can to finish the sixth, when one fell down and Astrid bent
down to the floor to pick it up. That was when she spotted something
under the old bed that she had been sleeping on. She pulled it out. A
wide smile spread on her face. It was a radio. An old one with a
broken antenna, but it was still a radio. She turned the button on top
to see if it worked and a crackling sound filled the room. She held her
breath while turning the button to find a station and cheered out loud
when the sound of Queen's "We Will Rock You" filled the room. It
wasn't a clear sound, but it was a sound.

*Finally, something other than the sound of my own tired breath or
the sound of me sobbing.*

She realized that the radio ran on batteries, but she had seen
stacks of batteries in one of the boxes on the shelves, so she should be
good for a while. She put the radio on the table, then sat down on the

bed and listened to the tunes and voices of a DJ so far away, yet so close to her that she felt like she could almost see him.

It was like a drop of hope in an ocean of despair. But it was enough for Astrid to get her spirits up again, to make her remember the world outside, and to keep her from losing her mind in the small, suffocating room.

10

2012

Victor was still playing in the yard when I returned to the house. Maya was nowhere to be seen. I walked out the French doors and looked at my son knee-deep in the piles of leaves on the ground, talking to the trees like he used to do to the plants back in our apartment in Copenhagen.

They like it when you talk to them, Mommy. They need company too.

It was okay, his doctor had said.

"It's probably just easier for him to talk to things that won't answer. People with light autism like Victor find it hard to be social and be with people. At least this way, he's not lonely."

"But he tells me they talk back," I had said.

"It's still okay. No harm in that. He just has a vivid imagination and that's not a bad thing. Let him. Just remember not to let him lose complete touch with reality. He'll be just fine. You'll see."

Other doctors hadn't been as positive. His school had claimed he was getting worse, and soon after, demanded I do something. They had given me pamphlets and phone numbers for physicians who knew a lot about his condition. They told me he needed all kinds of medicine, and basically scared the crap out of me. After that, I tried different types of group therapy and acupuncture and whatnot, but nothing had helped him. The fact was that he was living in a world of his own from time to time, and there were days I was afraid of losing him to it completely, but somehow he always returned to me.

As I watched him in the yard, I couldn't see anything wrong with him playing on his own, even though he was talking to the trees like they were alive. How could there be anything wrong with that when he was this happy? I was beginning to think I should have stuck with our family doctor's advice and just not overdramatize the whole thing. The so-called specialists didn't even have a name for what was supposed to be wrong with him. It wasn't Asperger's Disorder, it wasn't autism, it was something milder, but still interfering with his social skills.

Personally, I believed he was just sad that his father had left him. That's all it was if you asked me, but then again, I wasn't a doctor.

The wind had picked up, but it wasn't cold yet, even though it was September. It was what they called Indian Summer. Victor seemed to still be in seventh heaven, so I decided to let him play for a little more while I went in and did some more unpacking. I was happy to see that Maya had already taken her stuff, so I had only mine and Victor's left. I spent a couple of hours unpacking the kitchen supplies, then another hour or so in the living room, removing some of my grandmother's stuff and putting up my own pictures and personal touches. Later that evening, I called for a pizza and we ate and went to bed.

The next day, I continued where I had left off. After breakfast, I picked up a box, went upstairs to my bedroom, and opened it. I removed some of my grandmother's old books from the shelves and put up my own instead, then I arranged the old desk, placing my laptop in the middle.

The idea still lingered in my head. Everybody loved a good murder-mystery, didn't they? Maybe I could write one based on Mrs. Heinrichsen's story. My fingers were eager to start typing, and I turned on the laptop and sat down on a beautiful old hand-carved wooden chair. Even though it wasn't quite my style, I quite enjoyed the furniture my grandmother had left me. It was beautiful, very old-fashioned and a lot of it probably antique. An old, long case grandfather clock that looked like it was several centuries old chimed in the corner.

My computer made a sound and I logged in. Although I didn't have my own Internet connection yet, none of the neighbors' were locked or even had a passcode, so I used one of theirs for now. It felt good to be connected to the world again, and I started searching the newspapers on the web for the murder on Fanoe Island. A few popped up, but most of them just had small notes stating someone was found dead in a house here and that the police thought it might be murder. I couldn't find any other details.

"Guess it's not that big of a story when an old woman dies," I mumbled, and looked out the window.

I spotted Jack doing yard work across the street, still wearing that beanie of his covering his hair, and I wondered if he might be going bald underneath. I picked up my binoculars. He somehow reminded me a little of Victor, the way he seemed to be in a world of his own of some sort. I saw him run inside, then come back with a tray between his hands. He handed the tray to a woman in a wheelchair. She must have been there the whole time, but I just hadn't noticed until now. I watched as he started feeding her with a spoon. The food ran out of her mouth like it would with a small child and he scraped it off of her chin and forced it back in. He said something to her, but she didn't respond. Then she lifted her hand and planted it directly on top of the bowl, causing it to tip and the food to spill. Jack stood up and started wiping it off.

How old was this woman? I wondered. She didn't look very old. Was she his wife?

I put the binoculars down and decided I had done enough snooping on the neighbors for today. I turned back to the computer instead and scrolled through the articles some more. I found a small feature about Mrs. Heinrichsen, which painted her as a woman who had been very important to the locals on the island and was known to be a big contributor to the local church. She and her husband had raised the money to renovate it back in the eighties, when it was falling apart and there was no money. I sighed and leaned back in my chair. If I was going to write a book about this, then I needed something more. I needed the dirty details. And I knew exactly how to get them.

Before I met the father of my children, I had once dated this guy who was a hacker. He could get in everywhere and he taught me a little too, something that until now I had only done for fun and to keep up-to-date with it. But now, for the first time, I wanted to use it for my own benefit. It was illegal as hell, but I knew how to do it without getting caught. So after about an hour of trying, I managed to hack into the files at the local police station. Not that it was protected very well, I admit to that, but it was still part of a nationwide system that the police used everywhere. I found the report Officer Dan had written and I opened it and started reading. The station had received a call at ten past seven a.m. and Officer Dan had responded. A man working for Mrs. Heinrichsen was supposed to drive her to the mainland to meet with her lawyer, and when she didn't come out on her own, he feared that something might have happened to her, that she might have fallen and hurt herself. But nothing had been able to prepare him for what he saw, he said in the statement.

I opened the pictures from the crime scene that were attached and looked. What I saw made my stomach turn. The remains of an old woman lying on her bed. It looked like she had been cut open. On the wall behind her, the killer had written the number four in blood. I covered my mouth with my hand as I read the forensic report. She had bled to death in her bed. Apparently, some of the woman's organs were missing. The liver, the lungs, and the heart had been cut out and removed. The forensics team believed it had been done while the woman was still alive. I felt nauseated by the thought.

I leaned back and studied the pictures. I could hardly imagine the pain, and to think it had happened right down the street from me? Why wasn't it mentioned in the papers? I couldn't stop thinking about why her organs had been removed. Why would anyone want to cut out her organs? To sell them? Yes, organs could be worth a lot on the black market, but she was an old woman. Why choose her and not a young person with fresh, new organs?

It didn't make sense.

11

2012

A couple of weeks later I bought that bottle of wine and went across the street to Sophia's house. The kids had started school and both of them had had a great start. So far, Victor hadn't had any seizures or anxiety attacks. So far, so good, I told myself. We managed to get the rest of our stuff from Copenhagen transported to the island and—even though we hadn't unpacked everything—we were quite settled in by then. It felt more like home with each day that passed. Maya was still angry and slammed the doors now and then, but apart from that, we were having an almost pleasant time in the new house. I, for one, was thrilled to finally live in a real house, something I had always dreamed of, with a yard, and it was even close to the ocean. The house was old and clearly hadn't been very well maintained in the last years before my grandmother died, but it had been a beautiful house once, and I thought it still had some splendor to it. For example, the tiles in the hallway were pure white marble, and the effect was gorgeous. They were a pain to clean, but I didn't care much about that.

Fall had finally come and the winds coming from the North Sea picked up a lot, causing the last leaves to fall off the trees and leaving them barren until spring. I had done some exploring with my kids (Maya frowning on the backseat, seeming annoyed, or even angry, the entire trip) on the island, and had to say that its beauty had taken my breath away. The island was only sixteen kilometers long and five kilometers wide, so it didn't take us long to drive from one end to the other. It had three towns, the smallest was Rindby, then came Sonderho, and finally the biggest was Nordbo, where we lived. Well, really, my house was located just outside of the town. I had learned that the entire western shore was made up of wide sandy beaches and that the island had one heath and one small pine wood.

I put on my long winter coat and told Maya to look after Victor and come and get me if he woke up. The sun had long set and darkness surrounded Sophia's small house.

I knocked on the door and heard yelling from behind the door. The door was opened and a small face peeked out.

"Who is it?" I could hear Sophia call in the background.

The young face had ketchup on his nose and was smiling. "Mommy is coming now," he said with a mischievous grin.

"Now, that's a nice surprise," Sophia said when she saw me. I lifted the bottle of wine in the air and she looked pleased.

"Now, that's an even better surprise. Come on in."

The house was a mess, but it had a nice atmosphere to it. It was small and cozy. Sophia removed some clothes from a chair and told me to sit down. A clatter sounded from elsewhere in the house and she rolled her eyes. "Give me a minute and I'll get these kids to bed, then we can talk properly," she said.

It took an hour. Several times, one of them jumped out of bed and ran around, screaming, teasing the others, and making them laugh. I couldn't help but chuckle myself. Five kids. It was quite a handful. I found two glasses in the cupboard, then noticed the sink packed with dirty dishes. I started washing them up and putting them back in the cupboards. When Sophia finally came back, she took one glance at the clean kitchen.

"Wow, I really should have you over a little more often. Thanks."

I shrugged. "I'm not much of a cleaner myself, but it looked like you could use a hand."

Sophia threw herself heavily in the chair. "Let's pop this baby open," she said and looked at the bottle. We chatted for a few minutes about this and that.

"So, how're you enjoying your new house?" she asked finally.

"I love it. Victor, my seven-year-old, especially loves it, Maya, not so much, but she'll get there. At least, I hope." I sipped the wine and looked at the woman I hoped to make my new friend. I had been a little lonely in the big house with no other grown people to talk to. She seemed worn out, but who could blame her with that many kids and being all alone with them?

"It's a nice house you got there. I wouldn't mind having it. Might even be able to give my kiddos a room each. How many rooms does it have again?" she asked.

"Eight bedrooms," I chuckled. "I seriously don't know what to do with that many rooms. We only need three. I think I've been inside all of them, but I could be wrong. I swear sometimes I'm afraid of getting lost. I haven't even seen the cellar yet. I'm afraid to get locked in or something. Saw it in a movie once. Some woman moved into a new house, then was stuck in the basement because a door jammed or something and then she starved to death."

"Sounds like a boring movie," Sophia said.

I laughed. "It was, actually. But seriously, it's too big of a house for just us. I often wonder how my grandmother managed to not get lost."

"I heard she only used the downstairs the last few years. Slept in a chair in the living room. I think she even died in it," Sophia said. "At least that's what I heard. Maybe it's just rumors. I wasn't here. I had met a guy and we were on a trip to Skagen when it happened. We broke up while we were there. A little too overwhelming with five kids on a road trip, if you know what I mean. Anyway, when we got back, she had died. I never heard what killed her. Was it a heart attack or something?"

I shrugged. "I don't know. She was old. I never knew her, though.

My dad never talked about her. I always got the feeling that he resented her for some reason. But he never told me why."

"Well, a lot of people end up hating their parents. Me, I love my mother. She's the one who comes to my rescue whenever things get too bad around here. She lives all the way up in Aalborg, but every now and then she comes down and saves me from killing my kids. I owe her a lot. Without her, I wouldn't have made it."

"So what about all the fathers? Aren't they around?" I asked, and poured us both a little more wine.

"Well, I get alimony child-support from all of them, but not every month, since there's always one of them trying to avoid having to pay. But then I threaten to call the police and they always pay. It helps me a lot financially. I work as a teacher at the school on the side. Yeah, more children. Who would have figured, huh? You'd think I had enough at home."

"No. I bet you're great at it," I said.

"Well, it pays the bills. The days are short, plus I have vacation whenever my kids have it. But it also means I have to deal with them even when I'm at work," she said and laughed.

I nodded and drank some more. It felt great to finally talk to a grown up again. The wind made the old house creak. I could feel the cold from the window. Sophia saw it on my face.

"These houses are old," she said. "The ones on our side of the road aren't as fancy as yours. Used to be old summer cabins, but later, they were rebuilt and people were allowed to live in them all year around. But they are badly insulated. Can't keep the cold wind out at winter. I bet your mansion doesn't have those kinds of problems."

"I haven't lived in it long enough to know, but until now there haven't been any problems, no," I answered, feeling a little guilty for living in this big house all alone with my two kids.

"I thought not. Well, I made my bed and now I have to lie in it, right?" She lifted the bottle. "More?"

"Just a last one. Then I have to get going."

"So, what do you figure of that whole Mrs. Heinrichsen thing?" I asked, as she was pouring the rest of the bottle into our glasses.

"What do you mean?" She put the empty bottle down.

"Did you know her?"

"No one knew Mrs. Heinrichsen. She was an old bitter lady who was angry at everybody, apparently because she didn't have anything better to do. That's all I know," Sophia said. "We never saw her much. She stayed in that big mansion of hers and looked down on us all when she drove out of her gate in her old Mercedes. Like she was better than all of us. " Sophia paused, then drank. She looked at me once she had put the glass down. "Why are you interested in her?"

I shrugged. "I don't know. Just curious, I guess. They say she was murdered."

Sophia exhaled. "Why anyone would want to kill an old lady, I don't know. I mean, why not wait till nature kills her on its own? But on the other hand, I think a lot of people would like to see her dead. That's just my opinion."

"Like who?" I asked.

"I don't know. But ask down at the church. She practically ran that place. I heard rumors she even controlled the pastor's speeches and corrected them before he did his sermons. She used to be the chairman of the parish council, but it wasn't a democracy, as far as I know. Ran it like a dictator. Nothing was decided unless it came from her. So I guess she could have gotten a lot of enemies down there."

"Do you go to that church?" I asked.

Sophia burst into a loud laughter. "Me? You have got to be kidding. An unmarried single mom with five kids all from different fathers. No way they would ever even let me in."

"It sounds pretty old fashioned. Don't you think these things have changed, that they could be different?" I asked.

Sophia smiled compassionately. "You really are from the big city, aren't you? Out here these things don't change. Especially not when it comes to the Home Missions society. They are kings out here. Me, I'm not from around here; I just moved here with one of my boyfriends and then stayed when he moved away, so I don't care, but those people, they're like a closed society where you can't get access unless you are born here or you become just like them. And that means forgetting all about who you are, and forgetting all about having sex or even thinking about it. You keep those hands above the blanket, little missy. Those people still tell their kids that if they masturbate, they'll wake up blind. I kid you not. That's what they tell them at the church. That God will punish them for every wrong thought they have. I'm just glad my kids weren't born into one of those families."

"So, Mrs. Heinrichsen was one of them?"

"She was *the* one. She was their leader, the boss, the top, their freaking cardinal if they had one. She ran the place and decided who was in and who was out."

"Wow," I muttered under my breath. "It sounds like the dark ages."

"It *is* the dark ages, my dear. Welcome." Sophia laughed again. "I hope I'm not scaring you away 'cause I really enjoy having a normal person around for once. These women on this island drive me nuts. No wonder the youngsters get the hell out of here as soon as they're done with school." Sophia paused and drank. "All you have to do is to stay clear of those people, especially the women, then you're good. There are many nice people here as well."

"Jack, your neighbor, which category is he in?" I asked.

"Ah, Jack. Well, he's in a category of his own."

"How so?"

"He got out," she said and became serious. "Not many do. But it cost him dearly. Sophia sighed deeply.

"How so?" I asked.

"I think you'd better ask him that yourself some day."

12

1977

She felt the baby kick one morning while she was still asleep. It woke her up. Astrid started laughing. It felt like it was trying to tickle her from the inside.

I'm not alone after all, she thought. *You're really alive!*

Next, she thought about him. About Christian. Christian should have been here, she thought with great sadness. Been here to experience this wonderful moment when their baby kicked for the first time. No dad should be deprived of that joy of feeling his child for the first time.

Astrid told him she was pregnant a few days before she got stuck in the bunker. He would have been so thrilled to feel it, too; she just knew he would. Just like he had been so happy when she told him she was carrying his baby, that they were finally going to be a family. Well, not thrilled at first.

"Mother will kill me," he had answered.

Astrid had shrugged. "So what?"

Christian shook his head. "How did this happen? How?"

"Well, you tell me. You were there, remember?" She tried to touch him, to caress his chest the way he used to like it, but he pulled away.

They had met on their usual spot in the dunes. It was near the end of summer.

"But I thought we were being careful. I thought you were on the pill?" he said harshly.

"I was. Mother gave me those pills so I wouldn't get myself in trouble. A safety precaution, she called it. And they were supposed to work, they really were, Christian. I don't know why they didn't work. But it doesn't matter, does it? Things happen. Life happens."

"This is bad. This is really bad." Christian paused and looked at Astrid. "She's gonna say you did this on purpose. You did it to get me to marry you, to get a hook in me. Did you? Did you do this on purpose?"

Astrid shook her head. "I don't know what you're talking about. I don't understand."

"Of course you don't. You're too damn stupid to understand anything."

"What's the matter, Christian? Aren't you happy? This is our child. Made from our love."

Christian smiled. "Of course I'm happy. It's just..."

"What?"

He put his arm around her neck. "Nothing. You wouldn't understand anyway. I'll take care of Mother. Don't you worry. I'll handle this."

"What is it you'll take care of?" Astrid felt confused. She had been so happy once she found out she was pregnant. She was very young at only sixteen, but it was okay, wasn't it? After all, it was everything she had ever dreamed of, to become a mother, to start a family of her own and do it better than her own mother had.

"Don't you worry your pretty little head with that," Christian said and kissed her. It was the first and only time he ever called her pretty.

Then they made love one more time.

He was supposed to talk to his mother about it on the day everything went so terribly wrong for Astrid and she ended up in this strange hole in the ground. Now, she wondered if he ever got to do it.

She felt the baby kick again and she laughed, but soon the laughter became tears, tears of sadness and despair, when it suddenly struck her. What if she lived long enough to give birth? Was she going to do it on her own? Was she going to give birth to her baby down here in this hole in the ground? Or was she going to die trying?

13

2012

The Queen of Fitness was what they called her. Irene Justesen was her real name, but no one ever called her that anymore. Not after she became famous in Denmark for her fitness videos back in the early nineties and wrote herself into the history books as the first real fitness guru. There had been many others since, trying to accomplish what she had, but none had been as successful as she was.

Even as she was approaching seventy, she still looked as fit as ever and she still told people they could also get those iron buns if only they worked on it.

In many ways, Irene Justesen was a success story, one that many people admired and tried to emulate. She had made millions during the nineties. People bought her videos, her books, and she even had her own show on TV. *Iron Buttocks in Fifteen Minutes* quickly became one of the most popular TV shows in the history of television in Denmark. People everywhere in the country, tall or small, old or young, watched as Irene Justesen showed them how to *work those abs* or *get rid of the cellulite in only fourteen days*. The key to her success was being at the right place at the right time. She started making her videos just as the health and fitness wave swept across the country and everybody had to start working out. Plus, she was the first one. The first to make it easy for people to get in shape, to *Shape It Up* like the title of her first video. For the first time, people didn't have to go all the way down to the fitness center (of which there were very few back then), and they didn't have to join some aerobics class and sweat on a floor among twenty other people (who were always more fit and better looking), while looking at how ridiculous they appeared in the wall-to-wall mirrors. No, with these new videos, they could stay at home and work out. They could do it in private, where no one was looking. And that suited the Danes very well. Everybody had to have one of her videos at home, and often people would make sure to have the cover lying out somewhere in the living room when they had guests, just to be able to remove it, blushing slightly, with an *excuse me, I was just working out earlier today*. It was prestige, a symbol of status, of being a person who had things under control, and it made a great party topic for a change (instead of the weather, which seemed to have been debated for ages).

Her success lasted all through the nineties, when suddenly people began to find it embarrassing to have the videos and stopped watching the show on TV. Other fitness gurus came along and tried to do what The Queen of Fitness had done, but they never had the same kind of success she had.

But Irene never seemed to make peace with the fact that she was no longer popular. She still lived on Fanoe island, where she had grown up, but now she had bought a huge mansion, much to the island-peoples' discussion. She knew she was the talk of the town and she knew what they said behind her back, but she no longer cared. She had put the old lifestyle behind her and broken into a new life and she had done it on her own. Irene didn't need those people anymore, not after...well, not after what they did to her. She still thought she was famous and she did occasionally have a tourist or two come up to her on the street and ask her if she was the Queen of Fitness.

Now, she had decided to revive her career. Before it was too late.

At sixty-nine years of age, she made a new video, targeting the older audience, of course, and she was about to release it on DVD. It had been a long time since Irene Justesen had last felt this excited about anything.

After her downturn, she turned to drinking, and when that didn't help anymore, she started popping pills. Years of abuse made her realize she had been lonely for most of her life, and the only time she could remember being really happy was back in the days when she had been at the top of her career. Years had passed, and recently released from the latest bout of rehab, she was ready for a re-launch of her career. After all, people were fatter than ever out there. They needed her advice more than they ever had.

Now, she was sitting with one of her DVDs in her hand and couldn't help but shed a small tear. She'd had to pay for it herself: the making, the distribution, everything, and it had cost her far more than what she could afford.

The front cover showed her in a sports bra, leggings, and her trademark pink legwarmers, pink sweatband, and pink lipstick.

"Still looking great," she mumbled to herself, and considered celebrating with a glass of cherry wine that she had always enjoyed drinking. She poured herself a glass and looked in the mirror.

"You still got it, old girl."

14

2012

Irene Justesen was finishing her workout with a team of Nordby's old ladies, who had stuck with her for the last ten months, despite the general opinion people had of Irene on the island and despite the long break while Irene was in rehab.

Not that they had become any thinner during those months; on the contrary, but they liked coming there and it kept them from the pastries for at least the hour that the workout lasted in Irene Justesen's private gym on her property on the North-West side of the island.

Most of them thanked her before they went towards the showers. Irene nodded and thanked them back. They all thought she did this class out of a loving heart, but the fact was she was almost broke. She had spent a huge amount of money on rehab over the years and also on her latest DVD. She was in desperate need of money. Her lawyer had told her just last week that if she didn't start making some money instead of just spending it, she would lose her estate and the house within a month. Irene assured him that her next DVD would bring all the money she needed. She tried to make her voice sound reassuring and certain, attempting to cover up the uneven beating of her worried heart beneath her sweatshirt.

She was considering opening up for more classes, but wasn't sure there was enough interest on the island for that. Maybe she could do something for the tourists? Lord knew there were enough of those to keep her going for years. And they needed exercise while eating all that fried fish down at the harbor. Maybe they would buy her DVD as well.

Irene drank from her water bottle. She was out of breath after the workout.

Or maybe because you ended up drinking that entire bottle of cherry wine last night.

Irene coughed and sat down on a bench with her towel around her shoulders. She wiped off the sweat from her face and pulled off her pink sweatband. Her hair was soaked and her cheeks all flushed. It had taken all of her strength to do the entire routine and she had a hard time calming her heart down again.

Don't give up now. Don't give up on me, old heart. I need you.

The doctors at her last rehab center had told her she needed to stop it, stop the fitness or it would end up killing her eventually. In their opinion, her heart had become too weak from the excessive drinking throughout the years, and it wouldn't be able to cope with too much exercise or too much strain anymore. But Irene knew it wasn't the exercise that stressed the old ticker and made it weak. It wasn't the drinking either. It was that damn secret she was carrying, the one that had strained on her heart for so many horrible years now. But she had done the right things afterwards, even though it was too late. She had turned her back on those people, even though it meant she had fallen into disgrace among those who were important on the island. But it was too late. Way too late, before she finally stood up for herself. And that was the sorrow she had to carry for the rest of her life. A sorrow and sadness so deep it stressed her heart and she knew it would eventually wear it out. This secret of hers would end up killing her one day.

Irene sighed and got up to her feet. Her heart was calmer now, even though her pulse still felt high. She took her towel and walked towards the showers, where she could hear her ladies just finishing off and getting dressed. She opened the door and entered.

"Nice job today, ladies," she said, putting on her old TV-smile, the one that made her famous all across the country. The smile that was always the same, no matter if she was doing push-ups on the floor or jumping jacks. Or if she—like now—was in excruciating pain from knowing her past would soon catch up with her, one way or another.

"See you next Wednesday, ladies," she yelled at the women as they left one after the other.

A few minutes later, she was alone, her smile still stuck on her face like a mask for Halloween. Irene shook her head and sat down again.

"Poor baby," she mumbled, and suddenly longed desperately for a drink.

Irene stared at the floor for a few minutes. Suddenly, a black hairy spider came crawling towards her on the bathroom tiles. Irene put a hand to her chest and screamed.

"Gosh, you gave me a shock. Nearly killed me, you stupid creature."

Irene grabbed one of her shoes, then smashed it onto the tiles, killing the spider instantly.

Strange creatures those spiders, she thought, and put the shoe away. *Get in everywhere.*

She wiped the remains off with a paper towel and threw it in the toilet. As she watched it flush down the drain, she thought she heard steps behind her and turned with a gasp.

I was right, she thought, just before she was knocked out. *It was my past that was going to eventually kill me. I just didn't know it would be this soon.*

15

2012

Her head felt heavy as she opened her eyes. It was hurting badly from the blow she had received in the bathroom. Now she was back in the gym, and what was that? *Oh gosh,* she thought. *I can't...I can't move!*

A face appeared in front of her. The eyes...the eyes were so familiar. She had seen him before, but never up close. Oh, my God, could it really be?

Oh, but you know it is, don't you? You know who he is and you knew he was going to come for you one day. You knew all along.

"What do you want?" she yelled, hoping someone somewhere would hear her, but deep down she knew it was in vain. Her gardener didn't come till Friday, her cleaning lady not until noon the next day. By that time...by that time, she could be *dead.*

Oh, dear God. I didn't mean it when I said I wanted to go, when I asked you to take me home last night in my daze. I was drunk, dear Lord, I was so drunk. Now I'm sober and I want to live, I want to live.

"You know what I want," the man replied. He was smiling, laughing while looking at her tied up to the Total XLS Home Gym.

Her arms were attached to the machine above her head, her legs tied to the bottom. Irene growled.

"I have money. I can give you money," she lied.

The man laughed. His pale skin looked so fragile, almost see-through.

"I don't want your stupid money," he hissed.

"Nonsense. Everybody wants money. It's all anybody ever wants," Irene replied.

"Like you?" the man said. "Is that why you did it? Is that why you agreed to do it?"

Irene bit her lip while thinking about that time they had offered her the money. It had haunted her every day of her life since that she had taken it, but she thought it was for the best for everyone. How could she know what they were planning to do? The money had been enough for her to start her own business, a business that had given her a glorious career. Yes, she regretted what she had done every single day of her life, but she could hardly change the past, now could she?

She watched as the man danced around her until he stopped and pulled out a bag that looked like the ones the chefs had at restaurants. He folded it out and a big set of sparkling knives appeared. Irene gulped. It was all about playing her cards right now. This guy meant business, but maybe she could appeal to his soft side; everybody had one, didn't they?

"Please don't hurt me. I'll make it worth your while," she said with her famous smile.

The man giggled. "It's already worth my while. Seeing you suffer is all I have waited for."

"Surely, you wouldn't want to harm an old lady, would you?"

The man froze, then he took in a deep breath. He picked up a knife and a pair of surgical scissors. He lifted them both into the air and put them in front of her face so she could better see them.

Irene shrieked. She felt her heart pound hard in her chest. Sweat broke out on her upper lip. She knew it was a long shot, but she tried anyway.

"Sweetheart. I'm actually glad to see you. I have been so lonely ever since...since...well, I have been alone for so many years, and I bet you have too, right? We could start all over, forget the past and move on. What do you say?"

The man turned his head like an owl and stared at her without blinking. The grin was gone. He was serious now.

Irene swallowed hard. "What...do you intend to do with those things?"

"I intend to cut you open like a fish and take out your organs one after another. Then I intend to stuff that disgusting sweatband of yours down your throat before I leave you to bleed to death, if you're not already dead. How does that sound?" He asked like he was a waiter at a restaurant listing the day's specials.

Irene gasped and looked at the knife in his hand. "W-W-Why?"

He leaned over so she could see his entire face. Then he whispered:

"Because I can."

16

2012

I woke up to the sound of someone screaming. It took me a few seconds to get back to reality from my very weird dream about my dad, before I realized that the screaming actually came from within my own house.

"Victor!" I yelled and jumped out of bed.

I rushed into his room and found him crumpled up in the corner, shaking and screaming. I kneeled next to him.

"Victor, sweetie. What's wrong?"

But Victor didn't even look at me. His face was turned towards me and his eyes were looking at me, but he wasn't seeing me. It was like he was seeing something else, like he was still dreaming.

"Victor, you're having a bad dream, wake up," I said, and grabbed his shoulder, forgetting how he never liked to be touched.

As my hands fell on his shoulders, I immediately regretted having done so and pulled them away, but it was too late. The eerie screaming increased and was now followed by him yelling:

"No! No! NO!"

My heart was pounding in my chest and fear grew that he was going to have one of his seizures. We were far away from a hospital and I began speculating if they had any doctors on call or anything here on the island, since the nearest hospital was on the mainland. Victor's entire body was trembling.

"Victor, honey. Please, listen to me. You're just dreaming. It was just a dream."

But he wasn't listening. He stared into the room, his eyes looking like those of a blind person.

"Spider," he said. "Watch out for the spider!"

I turned to look and spotted a tiny spider on the wall. I exhaled heavily and smiled. "Is that the one you're afraid of?"

I walked to the bathroom and pulled some toilet paper out. I met Maya in the hallway with messy hair.

"What's going on? Why is Victor screaming?"

"Go back to bed, sweetie. It was just a small spider in his room. I'm removing it now so we can all get some sleep."

Maya made a frown. "Great. Now he's waking up the whole neighborhood over a spider? What a wimp."

"Just go back to bed, okay?" I said with a sigh.

Maya turned her back to me and started away, shaking her head. "Spiders. Tsk. What's next, a beetle?"

I stormed back into Victor's room. "Mommy's gonna remove the spider now, okay?" I said. "Then we'll all go back to bed."

I reached over and tried to kill it, but it was too fast. It crawled across the wall. Victor's nightlight cast a shadow on the wall, making it look much bigger than it really was. I heard Victor whimper behind me.

"It's okay, sweetie. I got it. Just need to try again."

Once again, I leaned over and tried to catch it, but again it was way too fast for me. I cursed out loud. "Shhh..." I paused and looked back at Victor. "Mommy never said that, okay?"

He didn't answer. His eyes were fixated on the spider trying to escape. I sighed and turned towards it again. "Third time's a charm, they say," I mumbled, and wondered why no one ever said that about marriages. I reached out and finally managed to grab the black spider between my fingers in the toilet paper. I pressed my fingers against each other as hard as I could to make sure it was dead, then opened the paper and looked at the remains. It had made a print on the paper.

"Kind of looks like a skull, doesn't it?" I asked, and turned to look at Victor, who had finally stopped screaming.

He didn't look at it, but kept staring at the wall. "No more spiders there, buddy," I said. "I'm going to flush this baby right out and then I'll be back to tuck you back in, okay?"

I didn't wait for his answer, but walked into the hallway and threw the toilet paper in the toilet and flushed it. Then I walked back. Victor was still on the floor in the same position when I returned.

"Come on, buddy. Back to bed," I said.

Finally, he looked at me with his wonderful blue eyes. "Mommy?"

"Yes, honey?"

"Can I sleep in your bed?"

I was startled. Victor hadn't wanted to sleep in my bed since he was an infant. And I couldn't imagine him being comfortable with being so close to another human being, even though I was his mother. I didn't know if it was a good or a bad sign.

"Sure, sweetie." I missed having him close to me. I missed being able to touch him.

Victor sprang up and ran towards the door. When we were back in my bed and I had tucked him in with his own blanket and put pillows up between us—his request so I didn't accidentally bump into him, I couldn't fall asleep.

"Victor?" I whispered in the darkness.

He didn't answer, but I could hear from his breathing that he wasn't sleeping.

"Why don't you want to sleep in your own room?"

He took his time. Then his small voice said:

"Because someone was killed in there."

17

2012

She hated cleaning the gym. Every Thursday, it had to be cleaned, and that was today. Clara wasn't in the best of moods when she drove the car into Irene Justesen's big estate. To be frank, she was pretty tired of cleaning, and especially tired of Irene Justesen, according to whom, Clara could never do anything right.

But she needed the money, didn't she? She needed that extra cash because her no-good husband had lost his job. That was over a year ago and he still hadn't found anything new.

"It's because we live on this stupid island," she had told him several times. "There are no jobs on this island. Why don't you go to the mainland and look for a new job?"

But all her husband did was to make fun of her accent. Clara was German and had moved here to get a better life for herself. She and Gerhardt, her husband, had met in Kassel, where she worked in a restaurant as a waitress. Her mother had been sick at the time, and Clara was fed up with taking care of her.

"Cancer eats more than just the patient," she used to say. "It devours the entire family."

Her father had left many years ago, and she didn't have any

siblings, so Clara was stuck with the old sick hag and didn't have enough money or education to move away. Where could she go?

Then Gerhardt came along. He was a lot older than Clara, but he offered promises of a life living on an island close to the ocean. Clara had never even seen the ocean in her life, and now she got to live close to it. Close enough to walk to the beach? She was thrilled.

But a year later, Gerhardt lost his job as a mechanic, and since then he hadn't worked on much else but opening bottles and emptying them.

Clara sighed and parked the old van in front of Irene Justesen's private gym. It was huge, she thought. How could anyone have a gym that was twice the size of Clara's house? It wasn't fair. The woman didn't even live in it.

Clara went behind the van and opened the back. She took out the mop and bucket and all her chemicals. If there was one thing Clara had learned while cleaning Irene Justesen's many houses, it was that the more chemicals she used, the happier Irene Justesen was. Simply because it smelled cleaner, Clara had learned. How it smelled was more important than if it was actually clean or not. Clara suspected that Irene Justesen was losing her sight with age. But she also knew her well enough to know she would never want to admit that she was, in fact, getting older. Irene Justesen would never wear glasses, not if her life depended on it. So Clara had learned how to cheat her and today she had planned to skip mopping the floor in the gym. She would just make sure the bathing area was clean and then clean the mirrors with her strong-smelling spray. That always did the trick. Clara chuckled. She could be back at the house and watching reruns of *The Little House on the Prairie* before lunch and still make a living.

"Beats going to an office every day and sitting and staring into a computer," she mumbled and found the key in her pocket.

She rolled her wagon with all her cleaning gear closer and put the key in the lock. She turned it and pushed the door open with her back first. She dragged the wagon behind her and reached to flip the light switch when she suddenly stepped in something. Something wet. She looked down. Was the floor soaking in something?

Clara smiled widely. It could be some water damage. Maybe a water pipe burst somewhere, maybe in the dressing rooms. That would be great. Then Irene Justesen would have to have it all fixed and that could take weeks. Weeks that Clara wasn't going to have to clean the gym. It sounded like music to her ears.

She leaned over and flipped the switch and peered into the gym to better take a good look at the damage, when she realized that the water she had stepped in was no ordinary water. It was blood. And not only was she going to miss *Little House on the Prairie*, she was also going to lose her job.

As she opened her mouth to let out a horrifying scream that would reach far beyond Irene Justesen's mighty estate, the last thought Clara had was that at least Irene Justesen didn't have to worry about getting old anymore.

18

1977

One morning, weeks later, Astrid heard footsteps close to the heavy iron door. She was asleep when the sound of life outside her strange suffocating world woke her up. Astrid opened her eyes and felt how her heart started pounding. Had they found her? Were they finally coming for her?

She ran up the ten steps and started hammering on the door.

"HELP! I'M IN HERE!" she yelled with all her strength. The emotions suddenly appearing were overwhelming, almost overpowering. Could it be, could it really be?

Thank you God, thank you. They haven't forgotten about me. They are coming. Someone is coming!

There was another sound from behind the door. Steps from between the two doors leading to the world outside that she had longed to see again for so long, and almost thought she never would again. She hammered her fists into the door again, crying, enjoying the rare feeling of relief that this nightmare was about to end.

"Please, help me," she cried, letting go of all her emotions, her sadness, her loneliness, her anxiousness tricked by the thought that she would never feel the fresh air again or see the ocean, that she was going to stay in here till her body gave up.

Astrid felt the tears running down her cheeks as she heard a rattle outside, the wonderful sound of someone unlocking the door and opening it.

A hand in the door, the beautiful sight of another human being. Astrid was hyperventilating now; oh, how she was going to enjoy being outside now, how she was going to look at the sky and watch the clouds dance, how she was even going to love the rain on her face.

"Oh, God, I'm so glad to finally..."

Astrid didn't get any farther with her sentence. Then she froze. The woman appearing in the door was well known to her. That wasn't what caused everything inside of her to freeze and all her hopes and expectations of being finally free to die. She even expected it might be her coming, since the bunker was, after all, located in her yard. No, it was what she was holding in her hand that startled Astrid.

"What...What...are you doing with that rifle?"

"Making sure you stay put," the woman answered, still pointing the rifle at Astrid.

"But...but...I thought...But...Why?" Astrid felt the desperation and despair once again.

"I have food for you," she said. "Food and water. Enough for you to get by for six months. Then I'll be back."

Astrid couldn't believe what she was hearing. "Six months? What...What are you saying?" She could hear the anxiety and panic in her own voice, still she tried so hard to look for answers, to understand. "Are you keeping me here?" The words felt like razor blades in her mouth. It hurt just to speak them. She couldn't believe what was finally sinking in. "Have you locked me in here on purpose?"

The woman didn't answer, but she didn't have to. Astrid wasn't among the brightest, but this she understood. Being threatened with a rifle was very clear. This was no accident. Her being locked up for weeks in the bunker with only canned food to eat was no accident.

The woman stepped backwards and pushed something with her feet. There were cans wrapped in plastic to make them easier to transport. Hundreds of small cans with ravioli, some with soup, dried fruit, cans of vegetables, meat, jam, and powdered milk. Behind that stood a pallet with big containers of water.

"There are some boxes of chocolate and some magazines in the brown bag on top to make the time go faster. You can drink the water from the tap near the toilet, but it doesn't taste very good, so I brought you some extra. And some soap to wash your hands. If you don't use too much at a time, it should suffice for a long time. There are also some new clothes and underwear in the bag, so you can change. You can wash the dirty ones in the sink," the woman said. "Now, pull everything down the stairs. I'm sorry I can't help you, but I have to hold the rifle, as you can understand. If you try anything, I swear I'll shoot you."

"But...?" Astrid's lips were shaking in fear. Spending weeks in this bunker so far had almost killed her, now she was expected to spend another six months? How? How was she supposed to survive? On canned food and bottled water? Surely humans needed more than that. They needed company, they needed fresh air, they needed a change of scenery from time to time. Could she survive down here? Did she want to?

"Why don't you just shoot me and get it over with right away. I won't survive anyway."

The woman sighed. "Enough with the questions, take the food or, as God is my witness, I'll shoot you."

Astrid knew the woman well enough to know that such a promise in the presence of God himself wasn't to be joked with. Not coming from this woman. Astrid nodded and started pulling the food down the stairs. It was heavy and her back hurt badly.

Once she was done, she looked up at the woman again with pleading eyes. It was hard for her to understand how anyone could be this cruel.

"Will you ever let me out again?" she asked.

"No."

Then the door shut with a slam and Astrid ran to it, hammering on it with her fists, screaming and yelling.

"You can't do this to me! Why are you doing this to me? You sick bastard. You're crazy. You can't keep me in here!"

Astrid heard the outer door slam and then there was nothing but that awful terror of silence again.

19

2012

I didn't pay much attention to what my son had said at night when I woke up next to him the following morning. All I cared about was that my beloved son was lying next to me, almost so close I could lean over and kiss him. Victor was still sleeping when I opened my eyes and I lay quiet next to him for a long while, just looking at him, putting my hand above his hair, pretending to be stroking it gently like I used to do when he was a baby. I leaned over and sniffed his hair. I didn't even get to wash it anymore, not since he learned how to do it on his own. Tuesdays and Fridays were shower days. Everything had to be so structured with him or he felt uncomfortable and insecure, the doctor had told me. So I tried to keep a schedule and make things easier for him, but it was hard. Today was Friday and I had to get him ready for school. Part of me wanted to keep him at home for the day and just spend time with him, but then again, I knew how important it was to him that everything was the way it used to be. And Friday meant school and shower. It also meant Disney cartoons on TV at eight p.m. and a small bag of candy. The way it always was. That was what made him happy, and if he was happy, then I was. I leaned over and whispered in his ear.

"Sweetie. It's time to wake up."

Victor stretched and turned to look at me. "This is wrong," he said and sat up. "Why am I in your bed? I shouldn't be in your bed. I should be in my own room. This is wrong, Mommy." He didn't look at me, but kept babbling on while getting his things together, his blanket, his pillow, his precious Pooh bear that he couldn't sleep without.

"You had a bad dream, remember?" I said. "You didn't want to sleep in your own room last night."

"I don't remember, Mommy. What did I dream about?"

"Spiders. Don't you remember?"

"But this is wrong, Mommy," he said, still while looking down. I could tell by the color of his face that he was about to have one of his attacks. "I am supposed to sleep in my own bed, in my own room. I'm supposed to."

"Take it easy, sweetie," I said with a calm voice. "It's okay. It was just for one night. You can go back to your own room again tonight. Nothing to worry about."

Victor's cheeks were flushing red. He was fighting to keep his anger down. "But it is wrong, Mommy. This is not my room. This is your room."

"I know, Victor. I know. Calm down, sweetie. It was all your idea."

Victor stomped his feet at the floor and started yelling. "But it is WRONG. Don't you know it is wrong?"

"There is nothing wrong with sleeping in your Mommy's bed, Victor."

"Yes, there is! When you have your own bed and your own room, then that is where you need to sleep."

Victor let out a shriek, then stormed out the door. I heard him slam his own door shut and start talking to himself real loud, scolding himself and probably me.

I bit my bottom lip and pulled off the covers. I wanted to just stay in the bed and feel sorry for myself. I wanted to cry, I wanted to yell into a pillow, but as usual, I did what was expected of me instead.

I took a shower, and then went downstairs to start breakfast.

Maya was the first one down. She came running down the stairs, threw her backpack on the floor, grabbed her glass of juice on the table, then drank it while still standing.

"I'm in a major hurry, Mom. No time to chat," she said, and rushed out the door. I glanced after her and watched as she disappeared on her bike heading towards town. I sighed and put bread in the toaster. I could really use some grown up conversation, and Maya was the closest I came to having another adult in the house. I missed chatting with her like we used to. I knew it was my own fault. I had neglected her the last couple of years, thinking she could manage on her own, and because I didn't have that extra energy to listen to her problems as well. It had been all about Victor since Michael left; she was so right about that. I started wondering if there was anything I could do for her. Maybe we could take a day off together? Go out and eat brunch, maybe? Do a little shopping?

"Where is my breakfast?" Victor asked, coming into the kitchen without looking at me. "You know I need my breakfast before I go to school, or I get cranky and can't concentrate. Did you make one toast or two?"

"Two. Just like you usually get."

Victor smiled finally and looked at me. I could tell he was relieved. Waking up in the wrong bed had somehow made him out of balance. It was unusual and he didn't like that.

"Good," he said and sat down. I placed his buttered toast on the table, while wondering if I should take him to a new doctor. Somehow it seemed like his—whatever it was—was getting worse all of a sudden. It had been going so well this far. Much better than in the city, why was he all of a sudden relapsing? Because of a nightmare?

20

2012

I drove Victor to school and then went to the grocery store afterwards. The lady behind the counter was too busy chitchatting with a colleague to take care of me. I had to clear my throat a couple of times before she finally noticed me and scanned my groceries.

Back at the house, I put everything in place, then unpacked the last of our moving boxes. I stood for a while and looked around the living room, deciding it wasn't too bad, even though half of the furniture wasn't mine.

"It'll have to do," I said to myself.

I grabbed a cup of coffee and walked outside to the yard. The wind was coming in strong from the North Sea and it made my eyes watery. I drank my coffee with my winter jacket on and wondered how great a view I would get if I cut down all the trees. But Victor would kill me. He had loved those trees from the day we got here. Even now when it was getting too cold to stay outside, that was all he wanted to do when he got home from school. Go outside and play with his trees. He could still spend hours out there talking to them, playing and doing God only knew what.

At least he was always happy when he was out there. I wondered if he ever saw any spiders and that was why he dreamed about them.

"One day, dear trees, one day I'll cut you all down and see what you're hiding," I said out loud, as if I also believed they could hear and understand. I considered walking down to the beach to get a better look at the view. I had only done it a few times since we moved in and it was beautiful. But it was a long walk through the huge yard and there never seemed to be enough time for something like that.

"I could do it now," I said to myself, but then again I really wanted to take a closer look at my research for the book. I hadn't gotten very far, but I really felt it would be worth my while to begin digging into the story of Mrs. Heinrichsen. So far I had written down a few notes about her, about her life here on the island, about what Sophia had told me, but I felt like I needed something a little more substantial. I had also found out that it had been twenty-five years since there last had been someone killed on this small island. And that was in a bar fight where someone pulled a knife. Before that time, they had no records. So you could argue that it was kind of spectacular that someone had been killed, like really murdered. It was actually the first real murder on Fanoe Island. I couldn't help but think that had to be a great story.

I walked back into the house and poured more coffee. I took it with me upstairs to the room I now referred to as my office. I had never had an office before, so it did take some getting used to, but it had a nice ring to it, I thought. Some days I just sat in there throwing pencils against the wall, saying it out loud.

"This is my office. I'm sitting in my office. Be right there...just gotta get something in the office. I'll get you the papers; they're up in my office."

Yup. It sounded real awesome.

I sat by my computer and turned it on, sipping my second cup of coffee. I realized it needed more milk, but I didn't have the energy to go downstairs again, so I drank it anyway. I found my notes and started scrolling. I really didn't have much, so far.

Maybe a piece of chocolate will help my brain think better?

I opened my drawer and pulled out the packet of Marabou-chocolate, my favorite kind. I realized, to my terror it was almost gone, and thought that maybe it was about time I started running. Then I ate the last pieces. I closed my eyes while the crunchy chocolate disappeared and made my taste buds have a party on the way down, flushing it down with the rest of my coffee. Then I looked at the screen. No. The chocolate didn't improve anything, but it sure tasted good. I savored the end of the sweetness in my mouth and opened Google. I typed something, then deleted it.

I yawned and leaned back. Fact was, I had no idea where to start or where to end. I had never written a book before, only dreamt about it a lot over the last many years, but it was a lot harder to actually *do* it than I had expected. I started thinking about where I really wanted to go with this book. I pictured it as a sort of portrait of the woman, Mrs. Heinrichsen, of her life leading up to her brutal murder.

Voices brought me back to reality. I looked out the window and spotted a couple of the neighbors gathering in the street. I couldn't stop looking at them. Sophia was among them. The strange guy Jack was there too, but was standing in his yard looking like he didn't really want to take part in the conversation.

Their voices were loud and sounded upset. I was curious and ran downstairs to get my jacket, quickly thinking up an excuse for coming outside at this exact moment.

"I was just on my way to the grocery store...what's going on?"

No, that wouldn't do. This was a small town, chances were someone might have spotted me at the store earlier in the day, or that the woman behind the counter could have told someone I was there.

"I'm going to buy some bread at the bakery for lunch?"

That would do. I decided that would be my alibi and it would be even better if I added a, "Does anyone need me to bring anything back while I'm there?" That would give me a plausible reason for actually talking to them, and asking what was going on.

Very good, I thought to myself as I walked out the door. Sophia saw me at once and waved. "Emma. Good, you're here. You need to hear this too."

"I was just going to the..." I realized they didn't care about where I was going or my fake alibi. They really had something important to tell me.

"What's up?" I asked, as I approached them.

Sophia looked serious and it scared me slightly.

Could it be something about my kids? Why did she say I needed to hear this? Was it Maya? Was she in some kind of trouble at her school? Or had something happened at Victor's school?

My stomach turned into a knot of worry.

"There's been another one," Sophia said.

"Another one of what?" I asked, feeling stupid for not getting it right away. I didn't know any of these people surrounding me, only Sophia, and of course Jack, who stood a couple of feet away from the crowd. For a second, I worried what they thought about me. Not something I usually did much, but for some reason I did suddenly.

"Another murder," Sophia said.

I felt my eyes grow wider. "What? Someone else has been killed? How? Who?"

"Irene Justesen," Sophia continued.

I could tell that the rest of the crowd knew all this already, since they were nodding along as she spoke.

"Who's that?" I asked.

A woman I had only seen a couple of times at the grocery store leaned forward. "The Queen of Fitness," she said.

"That's what they used to call her," Sophia took over. "When she was doing all those videos and the TV show."

I gasped. Suddenly I knew exactly who she was. We used to make so much fun of her when I was a teenager and accidentally flipped on her show. How we loathed those pink legwarmers and the sweatband.

"How did it happen?"

"I heard it from Anne down at the bakery," Sophia glanced over her shoulder, as if Anne was an undercover agent, whose identity was not to be revealed under any circumstances. "She told me the cleaning lady, what's her name...Clara Hermansen, found Irene in her own private gym down at the estate this morning when she arrived to clean it. Apparently, her blood had soaked the entire floor in there. And, get this...the killer had stuffed her sweatband down her throat."

Sophia paused for effect, waited for the people surrounding her to react. It came promptly. All the women gasped like they had rehearsed it. I turned and looked at Jack. He didn't take part in the gasping or talking. He seemed more like he was worried about something.

"Don't you think?" Sophia suddenly said and looked at me. I turned my head and stared at her. "I'm sorry, what did you say?"

"I was just wondering about two murders in a very short period of time on this island, it is kind of scary, don't you think?"

I nodded. "Yes. It most definitely is."

"Do you think they might be connected?" another woman asked me, like I had all the answers.

I shrugged. "I don't know. But I give you, it is kind of strange. Do you know if the two killings had any similarities?"

"To be perfectly honest, we don't even know that Irene was, in fact, killed," I heard a voice say. I turned and looked at Jack. He was the one who had spoken. He blushed when all the ladies suddenly looked at him.

"I-I-I'm j-j-just s-s-saying, we d-d-don't k-k-know, d-d-do w-w-we?"

His stuttering was all of a sudden back and I could tell it was hard for him to speak. But I was also relieved to hear that he could speak normally without stuttering. I remembered reading about how being put on the spot or in situations of pressure could make stuttering much worse. It made sense, I guess. I smiled at him and he smiled back. His blue eyes were gentle and very kind. I wondered about his story that Sophia wouldn't tell me. I really wanted to hear it, but was afraid of pressuring him or making him feel bad.

"Jack's right," I said. "We have no idea if it was, in fact, murder. We can't know for sure until the police also call it a murder."

"What about the sweatband, then?" asked a woman wearing a strange pink outfit with golden stitches.

"Well, I give you that," I said. "That isn't something she could have done on her own, but we don't know if that's even true, or if it's just a rumor, do we? So, until the police have confirmed it, I believe it's very important that we don't spread too many rumors, and especially that we don't make any new ones up as we go along. Fear and panic are very easily spread in a small society like this."

They all looked at me like I was a complete idiot. "That's just what I think," I said. "Now, if you ladies will excuse me, I have work to do."

I turned, feeling their eyes on my back while I walked back to my house. I heard steps behind me. Sophia caught up with me. "Are you insane?" she asked with a low voice, as she tripped on next to me towards my house. "You can't tell island people not to spread rumors. That's all they live for, for Christ's sake. It's what gets them up in the morning. Finally, something exciting happens on our island and you want them to keep quiet about it!"

I couldn't help but chuckle. The woman had a point. There wasn't much to do, let alone talk about, on this island. Two killings in less than two months were quite spectacular, especially since no one had been killed here in twenty-five years.

"So will you bring the wine tonight, or shall I?" Sophia said.

I laughed. Our weekly gatherings had become some sort of tradition already and something I was always looking forward to.

"I will," I said, even though I had been the one to bring it every time, but I also knew that it was fair since she was struggling financially.

"See you at nine."

21

1978

Christmas came and went, and so did New Year's Eve for Astrid down in the bunker. By January, her stomach had grown so big, she was out of breath from her daily exercise: walking fifty times up and down the stairs and the little bit of gymnastics she had taught herself to do on the cold concrete floor.

The radio had become her closest friend and helped her keep track of the days. Some days she would spend on the bench crying, others she felt strong and did whatever it took to keep living, to have some sort of decent life, even given the circumstances. She would keep herself busy with washing her clothes, cleaning the toilet, and reading her magazines over and over again.

But what Astrid loved the most was to simply lie still on her back and feel the baby growing in her stomach. She would cry with joy as she felt it kick or move in there. Every now and then, she was struck with fear and almost panic that the baby would never know anything other than this awful hole in the ground. She speculated a lot about the birth and what she was supposed to do, and as the days passed on, she grew increasingly anxious that something would happen to the baby, that it would die or get hurt while she was giving birth. Astrid didn't know anything about babies or births, but she had read a lot in the magazines that had been provided for her, since they were all about motherhood, pregnancy, and giving birth. It calmed her a little to read the stories from all the women who had gone through it, but she couldn't help thinking that they all—unlike her—had someone to help them. Doctors, nurses, midwives. Astrid would wake up at night feeling contractions, but not knowing what it was, she would fear that the birth had started. She would even scream for help some nights, fearing that she had to go through this all by herself.

"How?" she would ask into the room and hear the echo of her own voice as the only answer. "How am I supposed to do this?"

Astrid had always believed in God and she also believed he was there with her in that hole in the ground, and she had a firm belief that he was going to help her go through this. If anyone could, it would be him. But she had her moments of doubts, and they knocked her down like a hollow tree in a storm. There were days she would scream and yell at God for putting her through this, and those days were the worst. The doubt and the fear made everything so much worse for her. She had grown up knowing that God punished people for their sins, and she was wondering what she had done to feel his wrath like this upon her life. Yet, on the good days, she put her trust in him and in the fact that he believed she would be able to cope with this trial, that she could do it.

"It's my punishment for having sex outside of marriage," she kept telling herself. "You make your bed and you lie in it. There are no tears that will get you out of this. You have to do it. It's what God wants you to do. It will cleanse you from your sin," she repeated over and over to herself. For some reason, it helped her and made her stronger.

By the end of January, the woman came again. Astrid had speculated like crazy about what she would do when the woman arrived with the next shipment of food and supplies. Oh, how she had gone over it many times in her head. How she was going to throw herself at her and try to wrest the rifle out of her hand, or how she would use the flashlight, swing it at the lady, and knock her out. But by the time she heard the sound of steps outside the door again, Astrid was too heavy, too pregnant, and way too tired to even get up from the bench. She heard the door open and cried when she saw the woman's face appear. She pointed that damn rifle at Astrid again.

"Stop crying, for Christ sake," she said, when she saw Astrid. "No one feels sorry for you. You brought this upon yourself."

"Please, just let me out now, won't you?" Astrid pleaded. "I'm pregnant and the baby will come any day now. I need to go to a hospital."

The woman with the rifle snorted. "I can't help you with that."

"But why? Why do I have to stay down here? I've learned my lesson. As God is my witness, I have been punished enough."

"It's not about punishment," the woman said.

"Then what's it about? Why are you keeping me here?"

The woman pushed the supplies closer and left them inside the door for Astrid. "There, you can do with them as you please. I have put diapers in there as well. For the baby, when it comes."

"Do you really expect me to go through childbirth down here all by myself?" she asked, whimpering. "What if something happens to me or to the baby?"

The woman looked at her but didn't answer. "You'll find all you need in the supplies," she said instead, then turned as if to leave.

Astrid got up with much difficulty, holding a hand to her sore back. "Please don't leave me," she said. "Don't leave so soon."

"I'm sorry. But it's the only way." The woman took one last look at Astrid, then slammed the door.

22

2012

I did it again. A couple of minutes later, I could no longer resist. I had to check and see if this alleged murder of the Queen of Fitness had anything in common with the killing of Mrs. Heinrichsen.

It didn't take me long to realize it did. And not only by one or two things. It was literally everything that was in common. Like Mrs. Heinrichsen, Irene Justesen had been alive while her organs were removed. And, like Mrs. Heinrichsen, it was her lungs, heart, and liver that had been cut out. According to the forensics, the killer hadn't stuffed the sweatband into her throat until afterwards. I wondered why that was. Did he enjoy hearing her scream? It was the only logical explanation. I looked at a map of Irene Justesen's property and realized she could have screamed at the top of her lungs all night and still not a soul would have heard her. So that was probably why he had waited. He wanted her to feel pain. He wanted to hear her pain.

I shivered in disgust and tried not to imagine how much pain she must have been in for those hours while he removed her organs one by one, before she finally bled to death.

I scrolled through the document and felt sick to my stomach as I looked at the pictures. All that blood. But one thing kept me looking. One picture really drew my attention. On the wall of the gym, on one of the mirrors, the killer had written a number with Irene Justesen's blood. It was the number three.

I leaned back with my heart pounding. Why three? The number on Mrs. Heinrichsen's wall had been four. What did those numbers mean?

I googled the Queen of Fitness and found that the story of her being killed had gone viral all over the Internet. All the major newspapers had it, and on my Facebook newsfeed, people were all writing about her and posting old clips from her show. I guess she all of a sudden became some sort of cult figure.

I read the articles in the papers and recognized Officer Dan, who apparently had been the one they all interviewed. Probably because he was so handsome, I thought. Or maybe more likely because he had been the first one at the scene of the crime after the cleaning lady called the police. He looked great in the pictures. But what struck me was that none of the articles seemed to have all the info about the killing. No one mentioned the fact that her organs had been removed, no one spoke of the number on the wall, and not a single one of them compared it to the killing a few months ago of Mrs. Heinrichsen on my street.

"That was odd," I said out loud and closed the computer. I walked downstairs to begin preparing dinner, while speculating why that information hadn't been included anywhere. No one looked at the two cases and saw the connection. They all talked about her career, her many times in rehab, and the fact that she had lost a child, a daughter who had run off at sixteen and never come home. They never even suggested that there could be a connection or that the police might work on the idea that there could be a connection. It was very strange.

"What are we having for dinner?" Maya asked, as she walked into the kitchen.

I was still peeling potatoes and completely lost in my own train of thought. "Hmm, what was that, sweetheart?"

"I asked what we're having for dinner," she repeated.

"I'm making pork chops. I'm going over to Sophia's later. Could you keep an eye on Victor?"

Maya made a grimace like she was annoyed. I tilted my head. "Please?"

She shrugged. "Okay. It's not like I have anything better to do anyway."

"So, how are things at school? Have you made any friends?" I asked, hoping to finally be able to take part in her life again. Victor was playing in the backyard, and for once, I had time to actually listen.

She shrugged again. "It's okay, I guess. I mean people are a little weird out here. Definitely not like they were in Copenhagen, but I guess I could get used to it...eventually."

I smiled, but tried not to show it. I found another potato and started peeling it. "Any boys that are of interest?"

"Actually, there is a guy who's kind of cute..."

Maya didn't get any further before she was interrupted by a scream coming from the backyard. I threw my peeler in the sink and ran outside. My heart was pounding.

"Victor? Victor? Are you okay, buddy?"

The trees seemed to look at me with their dark eyes and branches reaching out ready to grab me. I never understood why Victor found them so fascinating. I thought they were really creepy.

"Victor?" I said again.

"Mommy?" he replied. I detected worry in his voice. He was afraid. Something had scared him out there.

"Victor? Where are you?"

"I'm down here. I can't get up. Help, Mommy. Help."

Panic spread in my mind and body. My heart was racing. Where was he? Why couldn't he get up? Was he hurt?

He sounds fine. He's not crying. Calm down, for crying out loud.

"Victor? Where is 'down here'? Are you all the way down by the water?" I asked, thinking if he had gone all the way down to the end of the yard, he was in big trouble. He knew he wasn't supposed to go down there on his own.

"No, Mommy, I'm in between the trees. Next to the big birch."

The big birch, the big birch, what did a birch look like?

Its long thin branches dangling in the wind gave it away. I ran towards the sound of Victor's voice. I spotted his face and ran faster. He was on the ground, but what was he lying on? Some sort of hatch in the ground?

"What happened here?" I asked and came closer. His foot looked all wrong.

"I fell, Mommy. I fell over this thing in the ground. My ankle hurts really bad, Mommy."

I looked at it and tried to move it. Victor moaned in pain. "Looks like a sprained ankle, buddy. We need to get you to bed, to give it a couple of day's rest."

"I can't get up," he said with a strained face.

I kneeled in front of him. "Victor. I'll have to pick you up and carry you back in my arms. That means I have to touch you. Are you okay with that? Can I do that without you screaming?"

Victor thought about it for a few seconds. Then he nodded.

"Good," I said and reached my arms out. "I'm going to pick you up now, and I want you to stay calm, alright?"

He nodded again with caution, like he was a little reluctant. I bent down and put my arms around him. I felt his body shivering when I lifted him up. He was stiff as I carried him back towards the house.

"Sorry, Mommy. I was just running when I tripped over that thing in the ground."

"It's okay, buddy. Don't worry about it," I said and carried him inside. I put him on the couch and put a blanket over him. Then I leaned over and kissed his forehead, something I hadn't been able to do in a long time. I was surprised to notice that Victor didn't seem to mind. It was a small step, but felt like a huge one for me.

It filled me with hope.

23

2012

I left a little earlier than what I had planned with Sophia, since I had something I wanted to do first. I put the bottle of wine in the car and drove down to the police station instead. I found officer Dan inside.

He smiled and got up from his chair.

"Doing the nightshift again?" I asked.

"Yup. I'm a night owl, so it suits me just fine. I like to go to bed in the morning and sleep most of the day."

"Sounds like a vampire," I said.

"I hear they're very popular these days," he said with a grin worthy of a vampire. "What can I do for you?"

"I was actually hoping you'd be here. Can we talk for a second?"

"Sure," he said, and opened the door so I could go behind the counter where he was standing. "Let's go over here, where my desk is."

I sat down in a chair in front of him.

"Do you want some coffee or something?" he asked.

"No, thank you," I said. "I won't stay long. I have somewhere else to be. I just wanted to get some answers to something that has been bothering me."

"Do you mind if I grab one? I have a long night ahead."

"No, by all means."

Officer Dan left and I heard him in the kitchen. He returned with a big steaming cup in his hand. He was still smiling. I could see his muscles underneath the light blue police shirt. "There," he said. "I'm all ears." He leaned over the desk towards me. "What did you want to know?"

"Well...uh..." I cleared my throat. "I'm writing this book..."

"You're writing a book?" he said with great enthusiasm, taking a long sip from his cup. "That's really interesting. I didn't know we had an author living on the island. What's it about?"

"Well, that's the thing. The book is going to be about Mrs. Heinrichsen and...well, the murder and...now that we've had another one on the island, I thought I would come and ask for some details about the two killings."

Officer Dan sat up straight in the chair. He looked at me mischievously. "I see. You're here on professional business. I didn't realize that. I better be careful what I say then. Am I in the book?"

"I wasn't planning on it being fiction," I said.

Officer Dan laughed. "Well, maybe I can be the vampire in your next book, when you decide to write something people will actually read."

"Very funny."

Officer Dan grinned. "Okay, let's get serious," he said. "What did you need from me?"

"I was just wondering about the two cases. Are the police working with the theory that the two cases are connected?"

Officer Dan took in a deep breath. "Between you and me, yes we are."

"But that's not what you've told the newspapers."

"Not yet. No."

I lifted an eyebrow and looked at him. "You're lying to the press?"

"Well, there's lying and lying. We're just withholding some information. That's all. Don't look at me like that. It wasn't my idea."

I chuckled. "Of course not, but why? Why don't you tell them the entire story?"

Officer Dan exhaled. "Because we are afraid of panic. This town, well the entire island, lives off of tourism. We don't want people to think it is dangerous to come here. That's all."

I leaned back in my chair and looked at him. "But it will come out eventually. Then what?"

"By then, hopefully, we will have solved the case."

"Or you'll get a lot of unintentional publicity, and not the good kind," I said. "I used to work as a reporter, and they don't like to be lied to. The police covering up a potential serial killer? Not a good headline."

Officer Dan shrugged again. "It's not a serial killer until there are more than three victims. And the other stuff is not my headache. As I said, I didn't come up with the idea."

"Then who did?"

Officer Dan shook his head and leaned his chin on his palm. "I don't know. I just follow orders. But a qualified guess is that it was the mayor and the chief of police."

24

1978

Astrid went into labor at night. It started with small contractions every now and then, then more forceful ones, and finally the extreme pain that kept rolling over her, making her think this was, in fact, going to kill her.

In the beginning, she tried to scream in a last desperate attempt to alarm the world that she was down there in this hole in the ground, in pain, in labor, about to have a baby.

"HEEEELP!!" she cried out whenever she had the strength for it.

But no one came. Soon, Astrid forgot her circumstances, her situation, and her surroundings, and she kind of went into a world of her own, where only she and her extreme pain existed. When her water broke and soaked the entire bed, she knew there was no turning back. This was it.

She moaned and whimpered and fought her way through every contraction, through every wave of pain, and every now and then she wondered if this was even normal. Was it supposed to hurt this bad or had something already gone wrong? Could contractions really kill you? Could they kill the baby?

Oh, God, don't leave me here now. Don't leave me, please don't leave me now.

She tried to look at herself like Jesus on the cross. The pain as something cleansing, something that God inflicted upon her to cleanse her from her sin.

In the midst of it all, she called out for her mother through her tears. But all she heard was her mother's voice from the day she had told her she was pregnant.

How could you be so stupid? How could you do this to us, do this to me? I knew you would end up destroying my life one day. Now look at you. What were you thinking? Having sex outside of marriage? God will punish you for this, my child. Mark my words. God will punish you.

Astrid felt another contraction and tried to embrace the pain that followed. She didn't scream anymore, nor did she yell. All she did was let the pain take her and her body to where it wanted to go, knowing the pain wasn't something she was supposed to fight; if it was in fact God's wrath upon her, then she shouldn't fight it, she should let it do its work in her till it had cleansed her from all sin. Wave after wave rolled in over her, and finally she felt an overwhelming pressure from inside, and as she followed it, she let it overtake her body. She suddenly felt something, felt something move between her legs. She looked down and realized the baby's head was peeking out. She whimpered and cried as she felt the last desire to push again and the baby slid right out of her and landed on the bed.

Oh, my God, oh my. Is it alive? Is it breathing? Why isn't it making any noise? Isn't it supposed to cry?

Astrid grabbed the slimy, bloody creature in her arms and held it against her chest. Her heart was pounding; why wasn't the baby crying?

Then it came. The most relieving sound in the entire world for Astrid. The sound of her baby screaming for the first time. Astrid looked at her baby, then cried herself, holding it in her arms, rocking it back and forth.

"You're here. You're finally here," she mumbled, while the baby continued crying. "I shall never be alone again. You and me, boy. We will make it. Together we shall make it."

Astrid found a pair of scissors and cut the umbilical cord. Then she put her baby on her chest and let him eat from her breasts until she suddenly felt like more contractions came, smaller but still strong. Finally, she gave birth to the placenta and she flushed it in the toilet. She washed her baby in the sink, then clothed him in the clothes and diapers the woman had given her the last time she was there. The baby cried and cried and Astrid believed it was still the best sound in the world. Finally, there was going to be life in this hell-hole. Finally, the silence was broken.

25

2012

"I met someone."

I was on my second glass of red wine when Sophia just blurted it out. Her eyes shimmered with excitement.

"Really?" I asked. "Who is he?"

"The chef down at the restaurant Kabyssen at the harbor. He's originally from the mainland. Moved here three years ago. Boy, oh boy, can he cook. Not that foreign food, no Italian or Chinese or any of that sushi stuff. No, good old-fashioned Danish food. Just the way my grandmother used to make it. With lots of gravy, meat, and potatoes."

I smiled. "Sounds great. How is he with the kids?"

"That's the best part. He loves kids. Simply adores them. More than he likes grown-ups, I get the feeling sometimes. You should see him with my children. He plays these crazy games and builds forts in the living room. He's wonderful."

"Wow. You sound almost like you're in love." I sipped from my glass, thinking about my meeting earlier that night with Officer Dan. I had to admit I kind of liked him. He had that charm to him, and it didn't hurt that he was good-looking, as well.

"Well, I just might be," Sophia said and winked at me. "Well, at least so far I'm enjoying his company. That's all. But you never know. I might end up like one of them housewives you hear so much about."

"Is it getting that serious? How long have you been seeing him?"

"Only two months. I didn't want to say anything in case it turned out to be nothing, you know? But now I'm kind of getting the vibe that he wants more. Yesterday, he talked about us moving in together, like it was something we were actually working on. *Once we live together*, he said. And then he talked about how much it would help me out to have two incomes in the household and stuff. I swear, I almost choked on my meatball. I had pretty much given up on the thought of ever finding anyone to actually be serious about. I thought that ship had sailed, if you know what I mean. But he's willing to take me and my five kids and all."

"Sounds like a keeper," I said.

"I know." Sophia smiled widely. She was so happy; I had never seen her like this before.

"So, has he been married before? Does he have any kids?"

"He has been married once before, but they never had any children. That was actually why he left, he told me. He wanted children and she didn't. She just waited seven years to tell him. Can you imagine that? All those years he thought she was off the pill and they were trying, but she was taking the pill when he wasn't looking. He found out when they started fertility treatments. The doctor told him. She broke down and told him that she didn't want to lose him, but she also knew he wanted kids so badly that she would eventually lose him if she ever told him how she felt about having kids, that it just wasn't for her. That's when he gathered his things and left her."

"Brutal. Who would do such a thing?" I asked.

"Who wouldn't want to have kids?" Sophia laughed.

I stared at her. "You're not pregnant again, are you?" I looked at her glass. She hadn't touched her wine at all.

She blushed. "Maybe a little bit?"

I almost spit out all my red wine. "You've got to be kidding me!"

"What? Stephan is so excited. He always wanted children. It's the last chance for me. After this one, I'm closed for business."

"I bet you said that when you had your last one, too," I said.

She shrugged. "So what if I did. This is different. Stephan is cute and nice and maybe...maybe the love of my life."

"Well, I guess congratulations are in order."

"Thanks," Sophia said. Her eyes shone like only a pregnant woman's could.

26

2012

Victor stayed home from school the next day. Not so much because he was in pain, more because I wanted to spend more time with him and I used the bad ankle as an excuse.

I pulled out our old puzzles that he used to enjoy doing, and for hours we decorated the kitchen table with them. It was nice to just hang out with him, but I couldn't get my mind off the two killings. I kept wondering what the two women had in common. Why did the killer choose these two and not someone else? They seemed very different as types. Mrs. Heinrichsen was old-fashioned, uptight as far as I knew, a woman of Home Mission, known as one of the strictest religious sects in our country. And Irene Justesen. Well, that was a completely different story, wasn't it? All they had in common was that they were both pretty old. But maybe that was all they needed? Maybe the killer targeted old women because they were easy subjects, because they weren't going to offer much resistance. Maybe he had some sort of mother complex, making him want to hurt women?

What else did they have in common? Oh, yes. They were both extremely wealthy. Maybe that counted as a factor as well. Did he steal anything? Not according to the police reports, but then why? What did he get out of killing these old rich ladies?

I was blank for ideas. The only thing I kept thinking was that if only I knew them both better, it would make it easier to write about them and maybe find the parallels. Did they know each other from somewhere?

Before I knew it, I had put Victor in the car and was driving through town, towards the town's only church. It was situated on a small street with lots of other houses, behind a small fence and the cemetery surrounding it. I took Victor with me, since he could walk fine on his own again. We didn't speak as we trekked up towards the main entrance. It had a white painted wooden door in the middle of the red bricks. The black roof seemed pretty new, and all in all, it looked very well maintained, even though it was from 1786.

"It'll only be a couple of minutes," I told Victor. I opened the door and we entered the old church. It was empty and I could hear the echo of our feet walking across the tiles.

"Wow," I said. "It's beautiful."

The church was decorated with old wooden ships hanging on strings from under the roof.

"Fanoe is a maritime island," a voice said behind me. I turned and saw a man—the pastor, I surmised—standing behind me in his black robe and white collar. "They are models of real old frigates. Some of these wooden ships are more than a hundred years old."

"They're beautiful," I said and pointed at one to get Victor to look at it. "Look at the details, Victor. Even the cannons. Look at those."

But Victor didn't look. Instead, he whimpered and grabbed my hand. I stared down at him while he clung to my leg and looked at the pastor. I stroked Victor's hair gently, wondering why he was so scared all of a sudden. But I was also enjoying the closeness that these last days had given me. I had to treasure them, since I didn't know how long it would last before Victor went back to being his old, untouchable self.

"You are new to the island?" the pastor asked and smiled at Victor. "Tourists?"

"No. We inherited a house here in town. Mrs. Frost's old house, after she passed away."

The pastor changed his facial expression. "Ah, I see. Don't think I remember you from the funeral."

Victor clenched my hand as the pastor smiled at him again. "No," I said. "We weren't there. I am her grandchild."

I wanted to explain to him that for some reason, my dad didn't tell me about the death of his mother, my grandmother, and the funeral before it was too late, but somehow, it wasn't something I wanted people to know. Mainly because I never quite understood what had happened between the two of them. Why they lost contact or why my dad kept me away from her for all of my life. It was something I needed to ask him about next time I was alone with him again. I knew it bothered him that I had inherited the house, and especially that I had moved here, back to where he had grown up. But he never told me why. I was getting increasingly curious.

"Oh, well, that makes sense," the pastor said. "Although I don't believe your grandmother talked about you much."

"I only met her once, when I was four or so. My dad and she were never close, I guess."

I paused and looked at the beautiful church. Victor still clenched my hand. I had no idea what was going on with him.

"So, did you know my grandmother?" I asked.

"I did," the pastor said. "She was a very important contributor to this church. A member of the parish council, as well."

"She was? I didn't know that." I didn't even know my dad had been brought up with any religion at all, but then again, I didn't know much about my dad's childhood. He never shared much about it.

"Oh yes. A very important member. We were very sad to see her go."

I nodded. "And then you lost Mrs. Heinrichsen recently," I said, getting back to the reason I had come in the first place. To get to know more about Mrs. Heinrichsen.

"Yes. Very sad. A huge loss to the community and to this church, of course."

"I can imagine," I said, wondering how I was going to be able to ask more questions without him finding it suspicious.

"And yesterday with Irene Justesen. What a horrible story."

The pastor looked at me startled. "Well, yes."

"Was she in this church as well? Did she come here?"

The pastor shook his head. "Not anymore. Not for many years."

"But she used to?"

The pastor sighed. "Yes, she did. But she left the church at the time when she started her new business. I guess she couldn't quite do all those things and still maintain a good Christian life. The love of money is a root to all kinds of evil, you know."

"Was she also a member of the parish council?"

The pastor looked pained. "Yes, she was."

"Did she leave voluntarily?"

"That is between her and God. Look, I have somewhere to be now. Did you come here to look at the church or are you interested in coming to our services? They're held at ten on Sunday."

"Oh. No. I came here because I'm writing a book about the two killings here on the island."

The pastor 's face tightened. "Do you really think that's such a great idea?"

"Excuse me?"

"Out here, we mind our own business. I don't think you should be running around asking too many questions, my dear child. You might get yourself into trouble."

I was startled. "Is that a threat?"

The pastor laughed. It was not nice laughter. It was condescending. I didn't like that one bit.

"No. Consider it a piece of good advice. Nothing good ever came from putting your nose where it doesn't belong. Now, if you'll excuse me, I have to go."

The pastor nodded and left. Victor's hand relaxed in mine as soon as he was gone. I hadn't realized until now that he was whimpering. "What's wrong, buddy?" I asked.

"Spiders," he said. "The spiders are coming."

I turned to look, but didn't see any. "There are no spiders here, Vic. What are you talking about? Victor. You're shaking? What's going on?"

"Take me out of here," he whispered. "Take me out of here now before the spiders get me."

Victor had a fever and was burning up by the time we got back to the house.

"Mommy, I feel so tired," he said with glassy eyes.

I felt his forehead. It wasn't good. I took his temperature and gave him something for the fever, then put him on the couch in the living room and turned on the TV.

I sat next to him with my laptop on my knees. I wrote down what the pastor had told me today. About Irene Justesen being a former member of the church and so on. At least I had found some sort of connection now between the two of them. They were both members of the church, of the parish council, but at some point, Irene Justesen had left. The question was, when did she leave the church and even more important, why? Could it simply be because of her career? I wondered who could give me more insight to how things worked in that church. At first I thought of Sophia, but I had a feeling she had already told me everything she knew. She was a newcomer like me and had never been a part of all that. I needed someone who had been on the inside and didn't mind talking about it.

"Mommy, my back hurts," Victor suddenly said.

I looked up from the screen. I put the computer down and lifted up Victor's shirt to better look.

"Oh, my God, Victor. Your entire back is covered in red blisters. How did that happen?"

Victor coughed weakly. "I don't know, Mommy. It was itching all night."

"We need to get you to a doctor. It looks like some of them are infected."

I put Victor in the car and drove him down to the island's only doctor. He had his clinic in his own house, a beautiful old red brick villa in the middle of town. I had called in advance and his secretary told us we could come in right away.

There were no other patients in the waiting room and we didn't have to wait long before Doctor Williamsen called us in.

He was a small chubby man with a nice smile. "So, how can I help you two? Something about a rash on your back?" he asked when we entered.

"There are a few on his arm as well. But it's worse on his back." I said, worried.

I helped Victor pull off his shirt. Doctor Williamsen walked closer and examined the blisters. Victor froze at the man's touch. The doctor noticed right away.

"He has trouble with letting people touch him," I explained. "His former doctor called it a light autism. He gets anxiety attacks from time to time."

Doctor Williamsen smiled and tilted his head. "Are you okay there, buddy?" he asked. "Is it okay if I touch your back?"

Victor hesitated, then nodded.

"All right. I promise to be careful. I won't hurt you."

"Doctors always say that before they hurt you," Victor said.

"Smart kid, huh? Been to a lot of doctors, have you?" Doctor Williamsen said, while studying Victor's back.

"Enough," he answered.

"I bet you have." Doctor Williamsen pulled away. "You can put your shirt back on." The doctor sat down behind his desk and took out a prescription pad. "I'm going to give you something to put on those blisters, twice a day. Do it in the morning and in the evening before you go to bed. That should help the infection."

"So, it is infected?" I asked.

The doctor nodded. "He has been scratching them and they have a small infection. That's why he has the fever. " The doctor kept writing on his pad.

"So, what is it? What caused it?"

"Oh, that? Those are insect bites. We get a lot of that on this island. Has he been playing a lot in your yard?"

"Yes. He loves to play out there. He likes trees," I answered.

"Well, there you have it. At some point, he's gotten too close to a bunch of insects and they have bitten him. He's not allergic to bees or anything, is he?"

"No. Not that I know of."

"Okay, then he should be fine."

"So, would you advise me to keep him out of the yard? It gives him so much joy to play back there. It helps him mentally, too. He has made a lot of progress since we got here, and I believe it's because of the yard."

"I see. Well, keep him inside for a few days until the infection is gone, and then I see no harm in letting him play out there again. Just tell him to watch out for bugs and don't roll around on the ground. Then he'll be fine. After all, it's fall and the bugs will be gone soon."

"I guess he must have gotten the bites yesterday when he fell in the yard and couldn't get up," I said and looked at Victor. As usual he didn't look at either of us, but studied some plastic skeleton that the doctor had in the corner. "He hurt his ankle and couldn't get up on his own. Is that when you got those bug bites, Victor? Is it?" I asked my son.

But Victor wasn't present anymore. He had gone into some sort of world of his own, like he often did, and now he was humming a song while staring at the skeleton.

"It must have been," the doctor said. He smiled and handed me the prescription. "Welcome to Fanoe Island, by the way, I hope you'll like it here," he said as we left.

28

1982

A strid had prepared everything. Sebastian was still asleep while she opened the cans. She was going to use one of the cans with tuna, since it was a special day and since this was Sebastian's favorite. Those and the ones with fruit cocktail. She opened one of those as well. Then she placed a small piece of chocolate next to the cans that she had opened. It was their last one and she had saved it for this day.

Astrid walked over and stroked Sebastian's hair gently, and then she kissed him and whispered in his ear.

"Wake up, sleepyhead. It's your birthday."

Then she sang the Danish birthday song and slowly Sebastian opened his eyes. "Good morning, sweetheart. It's your big day today. Four years old. You're a big boy now."

Sebastian smiled and threw his arms around his mother's neck. She leaned over and kissed him, feeling overwhelmed by her love for him. Her boy. Her entire world.

Ever since he was born, life had completely changed for Astrid in the bunker. Suddenly, she wasn't alone, and suddenly she had no time to feel sorry for herself or to think about her situation anymore.

It had been a great relief for her, but it had also been a rough couple of years.

The woman had brought her magazines and books about having a child, and every Wednesday she listened to a radio-show where some expert answered questions about children and bringing them up properly. That helped her along the way, but there were days she would break down and cry, thinking how much easier it would have been if she had someone to ask, someone to help her when things got rough, when the sleepless nights were too many and the room too small. She had cursed the fact that she had nowhere to run when the baby cried for hours and she couldn't escape it. Some days she would bang at the iron door again, in desperation and frustration. Those were the really bad days. Other days turned out to be absolutely wonderful. Those were the days when she never even thought about being locked in, when all she could do was stare at her baby, while breastfeeding him, stroking him gently across his soft hair, smelling him, loving him like she had never loved anyone before. This was unique, she had realized; she had never thought it was possible to love someone this much. But she did. And as the years went by, the mother and son grew very close, and like any mother, Astrid started dreaming of giving him the world. She wanted him to be able to go for a swim in the ocean like the boys in the book the lady had given them to read, the one he cherished so much and wanted her to read to him every night. Astrid wanted him to have everything a normal kid had, and it tormented her that she couldn't, that she was unable to give him everything he wanted. As he grew older, the questions multiplied.

"What's beyond that door, Mommy?"

"Why can't we go out of it?"

"Who's that lady giving us food?"

And on and on. Every year, it grew worse. Soon, Astrid wouldn't be able to avoid these questions any longer. Soon, she would have to tell him the truth. She knew that and had decided that today was the day. It was his fourth birthday and he was beginning to understand more and more. So far, she had been just teaching him letters and numbers and talking about the world outside, naming the countries and showing maps of where they lived. She had begun teaching him how to write and read and some math, and he was really getting good at it. He was a smart kid and he deserved to know the truth.

"So, Sebastian," she said, while they ate their food. Sebastian wasn't looking at her. He was playing with one of his spiders. Ever since he had been able to walk, he had been catching spiders in the bunker, keeping them as pets, playing with them like they were toys. They were the only animals he had ever encountered. The only animals able to get in and out of the bunker, either under the door or through the ventilation shaft.

"Sebastian?" she said again.

Finally, he looked up. The spider sat on top of his hand. Astrid had never liked spiders much and it always made her jump when he had them on his body. Sometimes he would even have them sitting on his face. It was natural for him.

"Yes, Mommy?"

Astrid looked at her boy. That beautiful creature who had changed her life completely. The only light in her darkness. She exhaled and then she told him everything. She told him how they were being kept from the world, trapped by that lady who brought them food, she told him about his father and how she had loved him, and about how he should try to escape if she ever died and the door was opened.

"If the door opens and you have the chance, you run." She grabbed his chin and turned his head to have him look at her. "Do you hear me? You run, Sebastian. Run all you can, don't let anyone stop you. And don't talk to anyone, don't tell them who you are or where you're from. Do you promise me that, son?"

"Yes, Mommy."

29

2012

Pastor Gotfredsen sighed, annoyed. He was sitting at the dinner table, reading his newspaper that was filled with stories about the death of Irene Justesen, the Queen of Fitness.

"Like she was ever queen of anything," he mumbled to himself and used his fork to pick up another piece of steak. It had been cooked too long and tasted horrible. The pastor shook his head while trying to chew the dry piece of meat.

"Melody!" he yelled.

The small woman came running through the door and stood with her head bowed in front of him. "You called?"

"You called, *sir*," he corrected her.

"Excuse me, excuse me, you called *sir*."

"Yes. Well, this meat is not edible. I doubt it is even suited for humans anymore the way you cooked it. Is that the way you cook your meat in the Philippines, Melody?"

She shook her head. "No sir. Had no meat, sir."

"Very well, then, but you need to do a little better from now on. I have my eye on you, Melody. You don't want to go back in the hole now, do you?"

Melody shook her head heavily and whimpered. "No sir. Not the hole, sir. I'll be better. Promise, sir." The small dark woman kept bowing as she walked backwards out the door. Pastor Gotfredsen snorted. He was sick of that woman. She could never manage to get the meat cooked right, or his shirts ironed properly. He would have to replace her in the morning. About time someone else had the chance to wait on him. He finished his meal: even the meat, since it was a damn waste to just leave it there. He tried to read his paper without reading the stories about the Queen of Fitness. But it was impossible. Almost everything was about her, her life, her career, her death that the police thought was a murder, but said they had no leads, not yet.

Pastor Gotfredsen didn't care who killed that woman. He was thrilled she was dead. Got what she deserved. But it did worry him slightly, all these deaths on the island. He couldn't help thinking that...*no, that's just silly. Just an old man and his paranoid thoughts. Stop doing this to yourself.*

Pastor Gotfredsen stood up from the table and walked into the living room, where his coffee and a glass of brandy waited on the table next to his favorite chair. Just the way she knew he liked them. He sat down and drank some of the brandy to try and drown out his worrying thoughts.

You old fool. You're happy that Mrs. Heinrichsen is gone. Now you have it all to yourself, don't you?

It was the truth. He was happy she wasn't there anymore. She had been too powerful for many years. And he had let her, hadn't he? In some ways, it was his own fault. After all, he was the pastor in a Lutheran church, but people from Home Mission had been too widely represented in the church back in the day when he arrived here. Little by little, they took it all over, didn't they? As soon as Mrs. Heinrichsen put her fat butt in the seat of the Parish Council and she was made a chairman, Pastor Gotfredsen never had much say anymore. She even corrected his sermons. Went through them with a freaking red pen every Saturday night.

But you never asked her to stop, did you? You never refused her the right to do it, did you?

Mrs. Heinrichsen had a way of making people do as she said. No matter what. It was in her voice, her look...such authority.

Pastor Gotfredsen hadn't been strong. He had given up resisting her power and found his own niche working for God. He was helping poor asylum seekers who were being kicked out of the country. He had taken them in, given them a home, and hid them from the government. Not only that, he gave them jobs. They worked for him.

Pastor Gotfredsen sipped the coffee. Then he exhaled deeply. "MELODY!"

The small lady stormed through the door. She bowed heavily and looked at the floor.

"This coffee is too cold!"

"I'm sorry, sir. Let me warm it up for you."

"No. This is it, Melody. I've had it with you." Pastor Gotfredsen grabbed the woman's arm and pulled her through the door into the kitchen. She was crying and pleading.

"Please, no sir. I be better. I be better now."

But the pastor had heard that too many times before. It was all about setting an example, teaching them, disciplining them, how else were they ever going to get by in this world? Those people coming to the country were so stupid, so naive and undereducated.

Pastor Gotfredsen opened the hatch in the kitchen floor. There was turmoil, someone yelled. Hundreds of brown faces looked up at him.

"Please, no!" Melody cried, but it wasn't enough. Pastor Gotfredsen threw her down to the others, and they grabbed her. Many faces stared at him with expectation. Pastor Gotfredsen pointed at one.

"You. You, there. Come up here."

A set of bright white teeth in a dark and dirty face lit up in the darkness. Pastor Gotfredsen reached down and gave her a hand, then he pulled her up and closed the hatch behind them.

The woman looked at him, then at the floor. "Thank you, sir. Thank you."

Pastor Gotfredsen snorted. "Go and clean yourself up, take a shower, then come into my bedroom."

30

2012

The new girl tasted good. After her shower, Pastor Gotfredsen had taken her to his bedroom and tied her down with rope. Her eyes were kindled with fear. Her lips quivered with angst. She was from Ethiopia. Been in Denmark two years in one of the camps where they waited till they got the answer from the government whether they got to stay or not. Her entire family was killed in her home country. Nothing there for her to go back to. Only death. But it didn't matter. Anisa still got rejected. She had to go back, they told her. It didn't matter that she had spent the last of her money to be transported in a container on a ship for weeks just to be put in a truck with hundreds of others and transported through Europe, almost being killed trying to get here.

Gotfredsen remembered when she arrived at his house. Like most of them, it was in the middle of the night. It was the same story. She couldn't go back because she would be killed. Gotfredsen understood that. He gave her a Coke and a smile in his kitchen, told her he would take care of her. The people bringing her in their van were workers at the Red Cross asylum center. Gotfredsen knew most of them by now, after all of these years of helping out these poor people. The workers trusted him and he trusted them. He would keep the people they brought to his house safe for a couple of years, then smuggle them across the border to a man he knew in Germany who would take them in and...well, Gotfredsen didn't actually know what happened to them after that, but at least they weren't sent back.

He smelled Anisa's skin again and started licking the inside of her leg. She was moaning carefully, like she expected him to get rough with her any moment now.

"It's okay," he whispered and put a finger inside of her. Still a virgin. Gotfredsen smiled, satisfied. It was rare he got them this young; what was she—fourteen? Fifteen? Who knew? It was hard to tell with their brown faces. It didn't matter.

But this one was special. He was going to keep her with him for at least a couple of weeks. Maybe even months. It was rare to get such a pure girl just for himself.

"Please, mister," she said.

He lifted his head and looked into her eyes. The rope was hurting her hands; he could tell it had scraped off some of the skin on her wrists. That turned him on. The way she was lying in his bed, completely defenseless, turned him on so much he could hardly bear it. She tried to speak again, but Gotfredsen put his hand over her mouth. She tried to scream, but it came out as muffled grunting.

"There, there," he whispered in her ear, while licking it. "I'll take good care of you. Just relax and enjoy."

His words made her fight even more. Gotfredsen watched as she tried to squirm out of his arms and pull her hands from the ropes. She was kicking and screaming underneath him. Then he laughed. He enjoyed watching them fight for it; it was one of his greater pleasures.

She was tight, even tighter than expected, and Gotfredsen closed his eyes in delight as he made her a woman. When he opened his eyes again to better look at her while she was fighting him, he noticed a small spider sitting on the wall behind her. He groaned and moaned as he pressed himself further inside of her and she let out a muffled scream underneath him, but he found it hard to enjoy it properly.

The spider irritated him. Gotfredsen growled and tried to close his eyes so he didn't see it. It didn't help. Just knowing it was there annoyed him.

He had always hated spiders. Ever since he was a young kid he had detested them. He used to pick them up and peel off their legs, one by one. Sometimes he would only peel off the legs on one side of it and watch as it tried to run afterwards. They were stupid insects that deserved to be killed.

Gotfredsen grabbed a pillow and threw it at the spider on the wall. The spider fell to the ground, then ran across the wooden planks towards the door to the bedroom.

"Stupid creatures," Gotfredsen said, and was about to turn to face the girl again, when he heard the door behind him open. For a second, he thought it was the spider, but how could it be?

He turned and saw the spider. It was crawling on a shoe. The man in the door bent down and picked it up in his hand. Then he let it crawl up his arm until it sat on his cheek.

Gotfredsen gasped. His body went numb. He crawled off the girl, who had stopped screaming.

"You? It's you?" he asked.

"My identity doesn't really matter, does it?" the man asked. "You know who I am."

Gotfredsen saw the butcher's knife in his hand. He gulped. "Can't we talk about this?" he asked.

"It's kind of late for that, don't you think?"

The man lifted the knife high into the air, then swung it and cut the ropes holding the girl down to the bed. "Get out of here," he said to her. "Get your clothes and run. Get away from here."

The girl did as she was told. She picked up her clothes one by one, while whimpering. Then she ran out of the room without looking back.

"You're not going to kill a man of God," the pastor said. "You're making a fool of yourself. You'll go to hell."

"Been there and back," the man said.

"Please. I'm just a pastor. I didn't have anything to do with it. I didn't make the decision. Mrs. Heinrichsen did. You were right about killing her. She did it. She was the one. She made the decision and talked the rest of us into it. Said it was the only way."

The man swung the knife at Gotfredsen with a wide grin like he was enjoying watching him plead for his life. Gotfredsen jumped off the bed and stood in the corner of the room. He climbed on a chair and screamed.

"I'm gonna get you," the man said, wiggling the knife in front of him like he was joking, kidding around with a child. But this was no joke.

"I assure you, I pleaded with her to not follow through with it," Gotfredsen continued.

"But you knew. YOU KNEW!"

As the man said those last words, he swung the knife again and sliced Gotfredsen under the kneecap. Gotfredsen screamed and fell forwards.

"You bastard!" he yelled. Blood was gushing out onto his hand. Gotfredsen felt anxious and started sobbing. "Can't we just find a solution for this? Isn't there another way out?"

The man burst into laughter. "I could lock you in the cellar and release all the servants you keep down there. How would you like that, huh?"

Gotfredsen shook his head. "No. No. Please don't do that. There has to be something else I can do. Something, anything?"

The man laughed manically. Gotfredsen picked up a lamp and threw it at him, but the man ducked down, still grinning. Gotfredsen's heart pounded hard in his chest. He looked at the door. Could he make it if he jumped and ran? Could he? He wasn't exactly young anymore and it would take quite the jump to get past the man, but maybe? After all, he used to be a high jumper in high school. But still. His knee was bleeding badly and hurting like hell.

"There is one thing you could do for me," the man said.

"Really?" Gotfredsen looked at him with a grain of hope growing inside, but the man's face told him it was too early to be hopeful.

"Yes."

"What?"

"Come to dinner tonight. Well I don't really need all of you, just small parts and pieces. Mostly your insides, really."

Gotfredsen whimpered, then glanced at the door again. Then he made a jump for it. He drew in a big deep breath and leaped through the air, his eyes fixated on the door to freedom in front of him. But as he was floating in the air, he suddenly felt something penetrate the skin just above his crotch. He looked down and saw the knife's handle sticking out from his abdomen, blood spurting out in the air.

Gotfredsen landed on the floor with a thud and never managed to get up again.

I can't move my legs. Oh, my God, my legs!

Gotfredsen knew he had become paralyzed by the stroke of the knife through his spinal cord and could do nothing but watch as the man started cutting him open.

I can't even scream. Please take me home now, Lord. Please have mercy on my sinful soul!

31

2012

The clerk ran as fast as he could on the gravel across the courtyard towards the rectory. *This is bad,* he thought. *This is really bad.*

He reached the wooden door to the pastor's residence and knocked. The clerk panted and knocked again.

"Pastor Gotfredsen?" he called. "You're late."

The clerk had arrived an hour before the funeral service of Irene Justesen. He knew Pastor Gotfredsen wasn't very fond of the woman for some reason that went far back in time, but the clerk certainly hadn't expected him not to show up at all. Now all the guests, the relatives, the friends, and the media were there, ready to listen to the pastor's words. All that was missing was the pastor himself. He had never been late to anything, not in the ten years the clerk had been working for him. Of all days, why today, when the eyes of the entire country were on them and the casket of the Queen of Fitness?

He knocked again, this time harder, almost hammering. "Pastor Gotfredsen?"

But still no answer. He grabbed the handle and realized the door wasn't locked. He walked inside. "Pastor?"

The sound of his voice bounced off the brick walls, but no pastor. This couldn't be? If he wasn't in the church, the pastor was always, *always* in his house.

"Pastor Gotfredsen? Are you all right?"

The clerk suddenly had an eerie feeling and ran upstairs to where he knew the pastor had his bedroom. He knocked carefully on the door before opening it. The clerk stopped. He cupped his mouth, but it was too late. Vomit spurted out all over his hand and the floor. The clerk whimpered and sobbed while looking at the gruesome sight of his pastor on the bed, smeared in his own blood, his chest cut open.

"Oh, dear Lord," the clerk said, then closed the door again. He stood for a while trying to catch his breath, trying to calm himself down and not hyperventilate. He felt dizzy, it was like the entire hallway was spinning around him. He couldn't believe what he had just seen. Whatever had taken place in there couldn't be human. No human was capable of such cruelty. Were they? None he knew of. He had heard of evil in the world, but never ever thought he would encounter anything remotely like this.

The clerk ran downstairs, crying, screaming, then stopped in the kitchen to look for the pastor's phone. He found it on the table and picked it up, trying to figure out what to say. He had never had to call for help before.

"Oh, God, you have to help me here, please help me."

As he opened the phone, the clerk suddenly heard a sound. He gasped and looked up. It was like a knocking, and now there were voices, too? Was someone in the house? The clerk gasped. Could it be the killer? Was the killer still in the house, maybe waiting for his next victim?

"Who's there?" he yelled.

He heard a bump, more voices, banging, someone yelling. What was that? The clerk stepped forward. He glanced at the kitchen knives on the table and grabbed one in his hand. He held it out in front of him as he walked closer.

"Identify yourself, please," he said.

Another sound. Someone hammering on something, like a door, muffled yelling. What was that? What could it be? Had he walked into some sort of trap? Was there an entire flock of killers in here waiting for him to come close enough, and then jump him? If so, where were they? Who were they? The clerk gulped and backed up slightly. There it was again. There was that sound once again. It didn't sound like a killer or anyone who wanted to harm him, it sounded more like...more like...like people? People yelling? People trying to attract his attention.

The clerk looked down and noticed a hatch underneath him. One of those built into houses during the war to keep people safe during attacks. Most houses on the island had them. Small shelters or bunkers under their houses either inside or in their yard.

"Hello?" he said and lifted up the hatch.

Hundreds of eyes greeted him, crying faces, torn faces, men, women, and children. The clerk gasped and opened the hatch entirely to help them out.

Then he started to cry.

32

2012

Victor felt better a few days later and went back to school. The blisters weren't all gone, but the infection was, and so was the fever. So I sent him off to school on the following Friday, hoping I could get some work done before the weekend.

As I drove back from dropping him off, I spotted Jack in his yard. I parked my car in front of my house, then walked across the street. I waved as I came closer. He smiled shyly and approached me on the other side of the Beech hedge.

"Hi there," I said.

"H-H-Hi..."

I could tell he was fighting to speak and wondered for a second if I should just leave. That was when I spotted the most beautiful painting leaned against the front of his house. "Wow," I exclaimed. "That's a wonderful painting. Who did that?"

I looked at his hands and clothes and felt stupid. All was smeared in paint. He smiled.

"You did that?"

He shrugged and nodded.

"Can I...?" I asked and signaled if it was okay if I entered his yard.

"S-S-Sure," he said.

I approached the painting. It was huge. Tall and wide. The colors were breathtaking. It felt like it was drawing me in, even though I didn't care much for the motif. A giant spider sitting in its web. There was still something alluring about it, I couldn't stop looking at it.

"This is very impressive. Did you really paint this?"

He nodded again, while wiping his hands.

"Do you have more like this?"

"Inside," he said, sounding more confident.

I walked in. It took my breath away. Hundreds of stunning paintings just like the one outside, each one more beautiful than the last. I laughed. "You're kidding me! I love these. They are gorgeous."

Jack smiled shyly. "T-T-Thank you," he said.

I couldn't help myself. I ran around in his house like a small child finding Christmas presents that I wasn't supposed to see just yet. It was splendid.

"Wow, Jack. You're just full of surprises, aren't you?"

Jack had a smirk on his face. "I try to be. C-C-Can I give you s-s-something to d-d-drink?"

"What are you having?"

"Elderflower cordial," he said.

"Hm," I said.

"What?"

"You didn't stutter. Just before when you said elderflower cordial. You didn't stutter at all."

Jack blushed. "I-I-I only stutter when I am n-n-nervous. Or when there are many people."

I chuckled. I liked the idea that I made him nervous. It was flattering. Jack went to the kitchen and brought me back a glass of elderflower cordial. "It's h-h-home made," he said, as he handed it to me.

"You *are* full of surprises, Jack," I said and tasted it. "This is good. You make it yourself? Or are you just trying to impress me?"

"A little of both, I guess," he said. "S-S-So how do you like it here on our street so far?"

I shrugged and stared at a painting. "Not too bad. No, it's actually quite refreshing to get away from the city. How long have you lived here?"

Jack sighed and drank. "My entire life," he said, as he put the glass down.

"The woman in the wheelchair, is that your wife?" I asked. "I hope you don't mind me asking."

"No, i-i-it's okay. She's my sister."

"What happened to her?"

Jack looked at me, then looked away. He became very serious all of a sudden. "Long story."

I found a chair and sat down. "I have time," I said. I knew I was being pushy and risked driving him away, but if I didn't ask I would never get the answers I needed.

"You sure you want to hear it?" he asked and sat in another chair next to me.

I nodded and drank.

"W-W-Well you better know the story s-s-so you'll know to stay away from the right people," he said. "T-T-The thing is, my sister and I grew up here on the South side of the town. My parents were a part of this church..."

"Home Mission?"

Jack looked at me. "How'd you k-k-know?"

"Took a wild guess."

"My parents both died in a car crash. It h-h-happened on the mainland. They had been visiting some friends."

I almost choked on my drink. "I'm so sorry. That's horrible, Jack. How old were you?"

"I-I-I...was twelve and my sister n-n-nineteen."

"Poor you."

"My sister was old enough to take care of me, so she did. S-S-She became my legal guardian and we stayed in the house and tried to live a normal life. Well, you know, at least continue our lives. But the church people wouldn't leave us alone. They wanted to control us, you see. My sister didn't want them to. They kept interfering with our lives and trying to make decisions about me, how I was supposed to dress and what school I should go to, and so on. But my sister was strong. She wouldn't let them. Finally, she got so upset with them, she broke out of the church. She left and told them we were out."

"What did they do?"

"At first, nothing. What could they do? But, after a while, they began coming to our house, telling us we were sinning against God and all that nonsense. It drove my sister crazy. In the end she was so sick of them, she contacted the police and got a restraining order against them. One of them had grabbed her arm and made a mark, and that was enough for the judge to give her it. Finally, we were left alone. Then one day, I was home alone, while my sister was at a friend's house, but she never came home. The next day, the police came to my door and told me she had been in an accident. A hit and run, they said. She had been walking by the side of the road when a car swiped her. She's been paralyzed ever since. Can't even eat on her own. By that time, I had turned eighteen and could take care of her. So I've done that ever since."

I looked at Jack. I saw such vulnerability in his eyes. I bit my bottom lip, wondering what to say to a story like that. "Wow." It was all I could come up with. "So, you think the church people might have been behind it?"

Jack threw his glass against the wall, startling me. It scattered all over the floor underneath and I jumped, frightened.

"I know it was them. Don't you think I know that? You don't leave Home Mission. You just can't leave."

I wanted to speak, but held myself back. Jack was in a very emotional state right now. Too upset to think about what he said. I didn't want him to say something he would later regret.

"Can I ask you something?" I said.

He looked at me with angry eyes and nostrils flaring. He didn't answer, but I continued anyway.

"Irene Justesen. Did you know her?"

"Sure did."

"She broke out of the church too, didn't she? Many years ago."

He nodded. "It was right after her daughter disappeared."

"But they never hurt her for leaving?"

Jack seemed to be calming down now. He shook his head. "No, they didn't. Well my guess is they owed her."

"Owed her? Why? For what?"

"I don't know any of this for sure, since I was a child when all this went down, but after what I've heard, I think they were behind the disappearance of her daughter. I think that's why she left the church. But I also think she had something to do with it. I think they were all involved, but Irene couldn't stand it afterwards. Couldn't look at them anymore. Between you and me, I think they paid her a lot of money to get rid of her daughter."

"Why would they want to get rid of her daughter?"

Jack scoffed. "Because she was pregnant. She was sixteen and pregnant. That's not good out here."

"What do you think they did to her?"

He shrugged. "Maybe took her somewhere to take the baby. Maybe they killed her. Who knows? All I know is, she never returned."

I finished my glass while a million thoughts ran through my mind. "Who was the father?"

Jack ran a hand through his thick brown hair. He looked great without his beanie on.

"I don't know. But my guess is it was one of the boys from the church back then."

33

2012

S aturday morning, the story of the pastor was all over the papers and Internet. The media had been present for The Queen of Fitness' funeral. The journalists had been in the church waiting for the funeral to begin, wondering why nothing was happening, when suddenly the island's police car drove up and parked in front of the rectory.

Immediately, they all ran outside, and all of them had the same interview with the clerk telling them that the pastor had been killed, that he had just found him inside, and that it *wasn't a pretty sight.*

An ambulance arrived later on, along with the island's doctor, Dr. Williamsen, who declared the man dead before he was taken away in a body bag. The papers all had pictures of him being carried out to the ambulance on a stretcher, and then statements from the police on scene followed. It wasn't Officer Dan this time; he was probably off duty, I thought, and read the statements from Officer Clausen, another officer working down at the station.

"We do not believe this is related to the death of Irene Justesen, the Queen of Fitness," he said. "Nothing so far indicates that it is."

After that, the journalists mostly focused on the many illegal immigrants who were found at the pastor's property, and many of the other stories in the paper were about how poorly they had been treated and how the system was inhumane to immigrants. Not one of them speculated about the many killings on one small island.

I leaned back in my chair in the kitchen where I was reading the articles on my laptop. I was in a state of shock. I had spoken to the man just recently, when he told me to stop asking questions. It felt creepy. This was actually a man I had known, that I had spoken to. It was suddenly really close. The killer was right out there, on this same island, killing people in cold blood. I might even have seen him or bumped into him somewhere. Maybe at the store? Maybe on my street?

Victor finished his breakfast and was playing in the living room. I told him to stay out of the yard a little longer, until his blisters were completely gone.

The air temperature had dropped, so hopefully the cold would kill off those bugs that had bitten him. I wanted him to be able to bundle up and go out there to play during the winter. It seemed to be so good for him. The fresh air, the nature, the exercise. It was all good. And he needed it. He always got so cranky when he had to play inside for too long.

I grabbed my coffee cup and walked into the living room, where I found him standing by the window with his nose pressed flat against the glass. He was looking outside at his favorite spot in the entire world.

I walked up to him and looked out as well, while sipping my coffee.

"I know you miss it, buddy. But the trees and the yard will be there next week, too. Then you can go out and play, as long as you're careful not to trip again."

Victor didn't react. He stared outside at his beloved yard. I felt bad for him having to be stuck inside for the entire weekend. But it felt like the best thing to do, even though it meant having a cranky son inside the house.

"You think we're getting snow soon?" I asked, knowing how much my son loved the snow.

Victor didn't look at me. He kept staring at the trees outside. "A storm is coming," he suddenly said.

"A storm?"

"A blizzard."

"A blizzard in October? Where did you hear that?"

"The trees told me."

"Ah, the trees, huh? Well, I bet they know before the weatherman on TV, right?" I said. I didn't want to tell him that they had said on TV this morning that the next few days were going to be calm and beautiful. Cold as hell, but calm. No winds at all. It didn't matter. In Victor's imaginary world there could be a storm, there could be many storms that I never knew about.

"Well, we better stay inside, then," I said, and walked back into the kitchen. Maya was still sleeping upstairs, and I didn't expect to see her before lunch, so I put the leftover scrambled eggs and other breakfast foods in the refrigerator for her to take out later. Then I sat by my computer again. I gained access to the police file of the pastor. It was what the clerk had told the press about it not being a pretty sight that lingered in my mind.

A second later, my suspicion was confirmed. The pastor had been killed the exact same way as Mrs. Heinrichsen and Irene Justesen. Cut open while still alive and then the killer had removed his organs: his heart, lungs, and his liver. But why? I simply didn't understand. I could understand why someone would hold a grudge against some of the church people; especially after the story Jack had told me... Suddenly, I froze with my cup in my hand. Jack! What if it was him? My heart started beating faster. I stared at the computer screen with all those pictures, then out the window, across the street to where Jack's house was. He had a motive. A reason to want those church people gone. And a good one indeed. Could he have done this? Was he capable of something that cruel? I lifted my cup and drank some more coffee. He had reacted quite aggressively when I asked about the church and his story. He seemed like the type with a dark side to him. You never knew with people, did you? But still...I could hardly imagine him cutting anyone open and removing their organs while they were still alive. It was so cruel, so barbaric. Could he do such a thing? I shrugged and put the cup down. Maybe. But why would he want to kill Irene Justesen? She had left the church just like he did. But maybe...maybe she was in on hitting Jack's sister before she left the church? Maybe she was one of them, maybe she had been doing horrible things and then she left the church because it was too much?

It irritated me that there was so much I didn't know, like when did Irene Justesen leave the church? What year? When did her daughter disappear? I didn't even know how old Jack was. I would guess he was in his late forties, but could he be older? Could he be in his fifties? Could he even be the one who got Irene's daughter pregnant?

I shook my head and sighed. Too much guessing, too few facts. I was making up stories now. I scrolled through the police file and the pictures, thinking they looked very much like the previous ones. I wondered how long the police were going to stick with their story that it wasn't a serial killer, that the deaths weren't related. It wouldn't be long before the press started wondering as well. I stopped at the last photo. The mandatory number the killer had left written in his victim's blood on the wall. This time it was the number two. I found my notes and looked at the numbers. Why was he doing this? Was he telling us something with these numbers? I looked at them again. Four, Three, Two...was he counting down? Like a countdown before a rocket launch? Four, three, two, one...blast off. But why start at four? Didn't those things usually start at five? I drank the last of my cup and almost choked when it suddenly hit me. I had seen something similar. On the wall in Victor's room.

I stormed up the stairs and ran into his room. I remembered when we moved in there that there had been something on the wall. It looked like it had been washed off, but some remnants had remained. Like a print, not very visible, but when you walked close to it, you could see. I had thought it was paint. That someone had painted it for fun, like graffiti or something. I had placed my son's poster over it just until I found the time and energy to paint the entire room. I hadn't given it any thought since.

Now I walked close to the wall and carefully pulled the poster down. I held my breath as I looked at the wall in front of me. Right there, on the light brown color, someone had once painted the number five.

34

1985

She was losing weight and could hardly fit into any of her clothes anymore. Astrid had been saving on the food for the last month, since they were almost out and it was almost time for the woman to bring them new supplies. But Sebastian was seven now and growing faster than expected. He had been eating a lot of food lately, and in order to not run out too soon, Astrid decided she could cut back and let him have what he needed. But after weeks of hardly eating, she had grown weaker and was tired all the time. She didn't have the energy to play cards with Sebastian or read all the books they used to. She slept most of the day now and tried to explain to Sebastian that this was just a phase. As soon as the new supplies arrived, she would be energized again and able to do the things they used to.

"But, Mom, I want to play with you."

"Just play with your toys for a little while. Mommy just needs a little nap."

Then Sebastian would go in the corner of the room and play with his spiders, which had become his best friends and only companions ever since his mommy grew weaker.

"The lady will be here soon," Astrid said every morning when she served him his breakfast.

She would repeat it again right before they went to sleep. "Tomorrow, Sebastian. Tomorrow she will come and we'll have a big dinner with all the food we can eat."

"Can't wait, Mommy."

But the next morning, she would stare at the iron door, expecting, hoping, that this would be the day when the woman arrived. Over the years, she had stopped looking at the woman as her warden and more as their savior, bringing them food at the right time, the person on whom their lives depended.

Right now, she couldn't bear to think about the world outside, or all the years she had lost, or even how badly she wanted her son to know all that she had known: the ocean, the blue sky, and the fields of corn. She simply didn't have the energy for it anymore. All she could think about was hearing that sound again, that wondrous sound of steps, of life on the other side of the iron door. The sound of the outer door slamming and then the creaking sound of the iron door opening. Oh, how she missed it, longed to hear it again. It was her worst nightmare to be forgotten down here in this hole, that the woman should lose her mind or even simply forget to bring them food in time. The woman had never let them down before. She had always come; they never knew precisely when, but she always came. Astrid began to think that she might have lost track of the days and maybe miscalculated when she was supposed to arrive. She counted the cans and realized they only had a few days of supplies left for Sebastian to eat. Then there would be no more left. They would have to starve until the woman came.

Astrid looked at her son and stroked his hair while he was playing. He lifted up his hand to show her the spider he had been keeping as a pet. Valdemar, he called it. Astrid let him have his fun, even though she couldn't stand having the spiders this close to her all the time. She never knew where they were and would find them in her bed sometimes, which made her scream. Then she would watch how Sebastian laughed. It was the only fun he got to have, so she let him.

Astrid looked at the calendar she had made and put up on the wall with all Sebastian's drawings. According to the dates, it was six months and three days since the lady was last there. She had to be on her way soon, didn't she? Astrid nodded heavily to herself. She had to. Usually she came a few days or maybe a week before the six months had passed. It was the first time she had gone past the date. Or maybe Astrid had miscalculated? It could be. Maybe she had remembered the months all wrong, which ones had thirty-one days and which hadn't. It was getting harder and harder to keep track of months and years, but she tried as hard as she could. Listening to the radio helped her a lot, since they often said the date and told her if it was summertime or wintertime or if it was leap year. So, she thought she had it figured it out all right, but now she was doubting herself. She stared at the door, feeling the hunger, the starvation in every cell of her body. As long as Sebastian had food to eat, they were good. But what if the woman didn't arrive in time? Would he have to starve as well?

Astrid couldn't bear the thought. She walked up the stairs to the iron door, thinking she heard something, hoping it was finally the woman arriving, but something inside of her knew that wasn't it. The sound came from further away, from the world outside. The faint world that had come to mean less and less for Astrid. But she knew that sound from back when she was still part of the world, part of the living on the outside.

It was the sound of an ambulance.

35

2012

I put the poster back up to cover the number, while a million thoughts ran through my mind. I walked downstairs, thinking about what Victor had said that night when he had the bad dream.

Someone was killed in here.

How did he know? There was so much I didn't understand about him, so much that I couldn't explain. Could he have dreamt about it?

I walked into the living room and found him still with his nose flat on the glass. I approached him and stood next to him. I wondered about my grandmother. Was it her? Had she been killed up there in Victor's bedroom? Was she this killer's first victim? Why? Why was she killed? Probably because she was part of the church. But did that mean she had been one of those women in the parish council? One of those who had done what they did to Jack's sister? And to Irene Justesen's daughter, whatever that was? Had she been a part of all that? And what about my father? Was that why he loathed her so much, why he never spoke of her?

I smiled at Victor, and then went back to my laptop. I searched the police archives and found a report with my grandmother's name on it. I opened it with a hard-beating heart. The pictures were the exact same as the earlier ones I had looked at. The same as Mrs. Heinrichsen, Irene Justesen, and the Pastor's. I felt sick to my stomach at the images and had to close my eyes. So, my grandmother had been the first victim. Number five. It didn't take a rocket scientist to see that the killer was counting down. So the question remained: who was going to be number one?

"What's going on?" the voice behind me startled me and I turned with a gasp to see my daughter standing in the doorway with messy hair and sleepy eyes. I closed the lid of the computer and tried to look normal.

"Nothing sweetie. Did you sleep well?"

She nodded and stretched.

"Come sit down. I have breakfast for you."

"I'll just have some fruit," she said. She never was much of a breakfast person. I found some apples and bananas and gave them to her. She cut them all up and put the pieces in a bowl. Then she poured some yogurt on top and began to eat.

"So, where is Vic?" she asked.

"In the living room." I poured myself another cup of coffee from the pot. I made one for Maya as well, and added lots of milk to hers. She had just started drinking coffee a year ago and wasn't sure if she liked it or not, but it made her feel grown-up, I guess. I put it on the table in front of her. "Thanks." She stirred the steaming liquid.

"He's sad that he can't go into the yard today," I continued. "Don't know if he intends to stand like that all day."

Maya chuckled. "Probably."

"I guess you're right. It would be something Victor would do."

Maya ate another spoonful. I enjoyed watching her. I didn't get to see her much anymore. She had made some good friends at her new school and they seemed to monopolize her a lot. I missed her.

"By the way, Grandpa called."

"Did he? I'm sorry I missed him. Typical of him to call on the landline and not on my cell. What did he say?"

"Nothing much. But he did say he was looking forward to seeing us all tonight."

Coffee spurted out of my mouth. "He said what?"

"That he's coming out here tonight. Why? Didn't you invite him?"

"I sure did. I have been inviting him out here every weekend since we moved here. I didn't think he would actually come. Wow. That is great news. I have so badly wanted him to see the place. But why tonight?"

Maya shrugged. "How do I know? He did say something about going to Esbjerg to look at an old boat he was interested in, then he thought he might stop by."

"Well I'll be...we need to clean the place up then. I want him to see it at the best it can be."

Maya rolled her eyes at me.

"That goes for you, too. I want your room cleaned up before he gets here."

"Mom. Grandpa doesn't care about those things. Have you seen how he lives? I don't think he has cleaned it even once since Grandma left."

"That's true. He doesn't care about those things, but I do. I want him to feel good here. I want him to like it and want to come back. I'll have to prepare one of the guestrooms, too."

"Pick one far away from me. Grandpa snores really loud. I want to be able to sleep, thank you very much."

I chuckled, and then froze. "Oh, God, I completely forgot."

"What?"

"I am supposed to have dinner at Sophia's tonight. I'm meeting her new boyfriend. He's cooking for us. Oh, no. She's been looking forward to this so much. I can't cancel, can I? But I have to. I haven't seen my dad in months. I can't just leave him alone when he just gets here."

"Why not? I'll be here. Vic will be here. You worry too much. He'll be fine with the two of us. Besides, he's been driving all day. He'll be tired."

I looked at my daughter uncertainly. Maya got up from the chair and started walking towards the door.

"Don't forget to clean your room," I repeated.

She turned and looked at me, ignoring my last remark. "By the way, he said he was going to stay for the entire week."

Then she left.

36

2012

I was busy all day cleaning up the house and preparing a guest room for my dad. He called again when he was halfway here, and I finally got to talk to him myself.

"I can't wait to show you the house, Dad," I said.

"I know the house," he grunted. "Grew up there, remember?"

"I know. But still. Now we live here and we have come to like the place a lot."

"I'm not coming to look at the house. Just to clarify. I am not happy about coming to that place again."

"Then why are you coming at all?"

My dad grunted from the other end of the line. "Because I miss you, goddammit. I miss you and the kids like crazy."

I smiled and held the phone tighter. "We're looking forward to seeing you. Drive carefully."

I hung up, feeling excited. I had missed him, too. Ever since my mother unexpectedly left him four years ago, he had become a bigger part of my life and we had become closer, even though he wasn't one to share much about himself or his emotions. As I recall, this was the first time he ever told me he had missed me. Guess he was getting soft in his old age.

My mom, however, was a different story. I had hardly seen her over the last couple of years, ever since she moved to Spain, where she was now living with this younger guy named Pedro. Well, to be fair, he was only ten years younger than her, but still. I never understood her decision, even though I knew she had a blast down there and had become a lot more lively since she left the old house in Ballerup where my dad remained. Every month when my mom called me, she always said that her door was open for all of us, but we had only been down there twice in the four years she had lived there.

"I cleaned my room," Maya said.

"Great. Could you do Victor's as well?" I looked at the big windows in the kitchen and realized that they needed a good cleaning, as well.

"Really, Mom? Can't he do it himself?"

"I've tried to ask him to several times, but I can't get his attention. He keeps looking out that stupid window at the yard. I wonder what's going on in that little head of his. He hasn't talked since this morning."

"Maybe he's just really smart and knows how to get out of cleaning his own room," Maya said, before she went back upstairs.

I yelled after her. "Don't forget the bathroom! The toilet needs cleaning up there."

I received a deep moan in return.

In the middle of the afternoon, the car drove up into our street. "He's here!" I yelled. Seconds later, I heard Maya's fast feet run down the stairs. "Grandpa!!"

"Victor!" I called. "Grandpa is here!"

I straightened my dress and opened the door. Dad smiled widely when he saw me. "Sweetheart! You look beautiful."

I walked towards him and kissed his cheek.

"Island living certainly becomes you."

I laughed. I knew Dad was just being nice. I had gained at least six pounds since we moved into the house.

"Must be all that fresh air," he continued.

"Maybe I'm just happy for the first time in many years. The change of scenery really helped. I needed it," I said.

"I can tell. How are the kids?"

"Grandpa!!!" Maya forgot all about being a teenager again and ran towards her granddad like a toddler. She had tears in her eyes when she threw herself around his neck. "I've missed you so much, Grandpa. How are you?"

Dad chuckled. "I'm good as always, dear. But, more importantly, how are you? Let me look at you. Hm. Seems like island living becomes you well, too. You are absolutely stunning, child. What is your mother feeding you?"

Maya giggled. I was surprised to see her reaction. I didn't know the two of them had gotten this close. But I knew they used to enjoy sitting in our old kitchen and chatting when we still lived in the apartment. A pinch of guilt hit me in the stomach. Had I deprived the two of them a relationship by moving here?

"Victor, my boy!" Dad yelled. I turned and watched Victor come walking out the front door. He was looking down at the ground as he walked.

"Victor. It's Grandpa. He has come to visit us," I said, thinking I wasn't sure Victor even knew what was going on.

"Come here, my boy," my dad said and Victor approached him.

My dad leaned down and picked him up before I could manage to tell him that Victor didn't like being touched much lately, depending on his mood. To my relief, Victor just laughed and Dad placed him on his shoulders and carried him inside, with Maya following in his wake.

"Watch your back Dad," I yelled after them, but knew they wouldn't hear me.

I picked up his suitcase and trotted inside after them.

37

1985

Astrid woke up to Sebastian pulling on her arm.

"Mom. I'm so hungry."

She tried to smile, but couldn't find the energy. She reached over and drank a sip of water. It had been her only food for weeks now, and she was feeling the effect of it.

"Not now, sweetie. I'm so tired. I need to sleep."

"But, Mom. You sleep all the time. I'm hungry. Can't you find any food anywhere?"

She had checked everywhere. In all the boxes, on every shelf, under the beds even, but found nothing. It was all gone and had been for almost two weeks now. And there was no sign of the woman who usually brought them supplies. Astrid was beginning to lose hope and was starting to think that maybe it was for the better. Maybe it was best for the both of them if they died now instead of spending more time in this hellhole. Eight years had gone by and enough was enough. Astrid had started to read the Bible again. In her every waking hour, which became fewer and fewer, she would try and read what God told her, read his words of encouragement, and little by little she was beginning to think that she would be better off up there rather than down here, to think that her time here on this forsaken earth was up and she needed to move on.

She spoke to Sebastian about it. Told him about God and about Heaven that waited for the both of them, about Jesus who would take good care of them, and how they would never lack anything again.

"Up there, you'll see beaches as long as the eye can see. You'll see forests and even mountains, rivers, and lakes. You'll get to see all that you've missed out on while wasting your life in this hole," she said.

"But...but," Sebastian faltered with tears in his eyes. "But I haven't even seen this world."

"True. But up there...oh, gosh. You won't believe it. Up there you'll see splendor beyond anything you'll ever see down here. This world is evil. It's not worth spending your time on. You're lucky, in fact. You're very lucky, Sebastian, that you never have to be a part of this world. It's simply not worth it."

"But I want to," he argued in a thick voice. "I dream about what is out there behind that door. I dream of one day seeing it."

Astrid sighed and closed her eyes. They had been open for too long. She was getting exhausted just from the effort of staying awake.

"Maybe you will, Sebastian," she said, while drifting away shortly, then returning.

"Mom. I don't want to die in here. I don't!" Sebastian screamed hysterically.

"Not now, sweetie. I'm so tired. Mommy is so...so...so tired."

"Mom!! Don't fall asleep, Mommy. Don't fall asleep again."

"Mmm...Sure. I won't. Don't worry. Mommy will take care of it. Don't you worry, sweetie. Mommy's got it."

Astrid dozed off again, then felt someone pulling her arm hard and woke up again. It was hard to breathe. Like it was too much effort, like she didn't have the strength anymore.

"Mommy!!! You're not breathing. Please don't die," Sebastian was crying in the distance, but Astrid couldn't find the strength to open her eyes anymore, she didn't even want to; she didn't care about anything anymore as she drifted off into that sea of light in front of her.

She could still hear Sebastian screaming behind her as she stepped towards that wonderful bright light and the voices calling her name.

See you there, Sebastian. See you when you get there.

38

2012

"I hate to leave you like this when you've only just arrived," I said to Dad and kissed his cheek.

He was sitting in an armchair by the fireplace in the living room with a book folded in his lap that he had been reading to the kids earlier. Now he had dozed off and was half asleep when I had to leave.

"Pah. I'll be fine. The kiddos and me will have a great time. Besides, I'll stay all week, so we'll have plenty of time to spend together." He grabbed my arm and held it tight. "Don't be like your mother. Don't worry too much."

"She hardly seems like she worries about anything lately," I said.

Dad shook his head. "Don't be angry with her for wanting to have some fun. If this is what she wants, then let her have it."

"Wow. That's really big of you," I said.

He shrugged. "Well, what can I say? When you've been married this long, all you want is for the other partner to be happy. Besides, I'm doing fine on my own. Haven't learned to cook yet, but who knows, maybe that'll come one day, too, huh? Otherwise, they have great takeout places in Ballerup. I lack nothing."

He gave me one of those reassuring smiles that I knew he didn't really mean, but told me he didn't want me to worry anymore.

I nodded and gave him another kiss. "Okay, then. I'll be across the street if you need anything. Don't let the kids fool you."

"Ha, ha. I won't."

"Dinner is on the counter. Just microwave it and you're good to go. Victor won't let you touch his food or cut it or anything. He wants to arrange it first on the plate before he starts to eat. He doesn't like any of the food touching each other. He's very particular about that. It takes a while, but just let him..."

My dad grabbed my arm and pulled me closer. Then he kissed me. "Don't worry, honey. I got it. Even Victor. He'll be fine with me. Go have fun at your neighbor's."

"Okay. I will. See you later."

"Don't think I'll be waiting up for you, though. I'm beat."

"See you tomorrow, then."

My dad returned to his book and lifted his arm in a small wave. I took one last glance at him, then walked out the door, yelling to Maya and Victor that I was leaving.

"Good," my daughter yelled back.

I closed the door and walked across the street, thinking how much surprisingly better my children seemed to be doing, now that their granddad was in the house. I hadn't expected that at all. It felt good. It felt like we were a real family again. I could get used to that.

I knocked at Sophia's door and she opened it and ushered me in. I showed her the wine I had brought.

"Nothing for me," she said, and pointed at her stomach. "Remember?"

"I do. But I thought that guy of yours might like a glass or two."

"Sure. He would love it." She leaned closer and whispered, "He's in the kitchen, cooking for us."

Sophia pointed through the half open door and I spotted a tall, muscular guy wearing a white apron. He looked like he was a magician performing a very difficult trick. Sophia pulled me into the room.

"Our guest of honor has arrived," she said. "This is Emma. Emma, this is Stephan."

"Pleased to meet you," he said. He wiped his hand on his apron, and then reached it out towards me.

"Nice to meet you," I said, accepting his firm handshake, then looked at the many pots and pans he had simmering on the stovetop. "Looking good."

Stephan smiled, then threw some more spices into one of the dishes. Sophia pulled me away. "Come. Let's talk while he cooks. The kids are all in bed already. I managed to get them to sleep early tonight. Can you believe it?"

"No. Not really," I said. I really couldn't. Usually they were still running all over the place at this time. "Good for you."

"I know. I just have all this new energy. It's like I have gotten a whole new perspective on life. I'm so much more positive. Stephan has that affect on me. And on the kids. They are so happy when he's around. You won't believe it. He even helped me get them to bed. Sit down. I'll open your wine."

"Thanks," I said, and found a chair to sit in while she poured me a glass full of the fragrant red wine.

"Now," Sophia said and sat down on the other side of the table. "Let's chat. But before you say anything, let's talk about Stephan. Isn't he handsome?"

"He is, yes, I guess." He was, but not really my type. I couldn't put my finger on it, but there was something. Maybe the tattoos or the big muscles. It was a little too much, I thought.

"I guess?" Sophia said with a smirk. "Come on, woman. He's gorgeous!"

"Okay, then, yes. He is very handsome. Good for you."

"This kid is going to be stunning. I just know it," she said and held a hand to her stomach. It still wasn't visible yet.

"I bet."

I drank from my glass and looked at my happy friend. "So, is he moving in soon, or what's going on?"

"Next week," she said, flashing her pretty smile. It was wonderful to see her this happy. "So what's new with you?" she asked.

"My dad arrived today."

"That's good news, right?" Sophia asked. "I mean, you've wanted for him to come for a long time, right?"

"Yes. I'm really happy that he finally did. The kids are ecstatic. Well, mostly Maya, but still. It's great to see them with him."

Sophia looked at me questioningly. "But something is bothering you, isn't it? You seem like you have something on your mind."

I drank some more wine, then looked at Sophia. "Well I figured something out. I haven't told anyone this yet."

Sophia became serious. "Wow. It sounds bad. Is it? Is it something bad?"

"I have a feeling that it might be. I don't quite know how to wrap my head around it, but something is wrong."

"Well, spill it, sister."

I sipped my wine again. Wonderful smells were beginning to come from the kitchen. I was hungry, I realized. "I think there is a serial killer on the loose on the island. I have checked the police files and all the killings lately have been done in the same manner. All the victims have been opened up and their organs cut out while they were still alive."

Sophia looked at me and wrinkled her forehead. "But I thought the police said there was no connection between the three killings. Naturally, I suspected that there was. I'm not that big of an idiot, but why are they saying there isn't?"

"To avoid creating panic. They're afraid of scaring off the tourists."

"That would be bad, all right," Sophia said. "Without the tourists, we would go broke; the entire island would go broke." She twined her fingers and leaned back. "So, the police are covering it up for as long as possible, what's so bad about that?"

"There's more."

"I had a feeling there would be."

"My grandmother was one of the victims. The killer has been painting numbers on the walls of his victims, and I found a number on Victor's wall, as well. The house had been cleaned and it was almost gone, but I could still see it. I found her file and realized she had been killed in the exact same way as the three others."

"Oh, boy," Sophia said and grabbed the wine bottle. "You need a little more of this, I think," she said and poured some into my glass.

"Dinner is served," Stephan interrupted, poking his head into the living room.

"Oh, boy," Sophia said again and got up from her chair. "I've been waiting for this all day!"

39

2012

Everything was arranged so nicely when we got back into the kitchen. Stephan had set the table very neatly with yellow napkins and flowers. Every plate had food on it, arranged nicely with a piece of meat, two potatoes and some sauce, a small stalk of parsley, some roasted walnuts, soft fried onions, and pickles.

"It smells so good," I said and sat down.

"It really does." Sophia kissed Stephan on the cheek. "You're in for a real treat, Emma. Stephan is the best cook."

It looked really intriguing and I was famished. I hadn't had time for lunch because of all that cleaning I had to do. Stephan poured me some more wine. I decided it had to be my last glass. Wine on an empty stomach was never a great idea.

"So, Emma. Sophia tells me you're a writer." Stephan grabbed the chair across from me and sat down. I was so hungry now; I wanted to dig in right away, but to be polite I waited.

"Yes. Well, I have mostly been a print reporter over the past several years for various magazines. Before that, I did a little TV journalism for a few years, but I enjoy the writing more than that."

"Let me get us all some water," Sophia said, and left the table to fill a jug from the tap.

"And you're writing a book now?" Stephan asked.

"Yeah. Well...uh, I'm trying to. I haven't quite started writing yet. Right now I'm mostly doing research."

"Sophia tells me it's about the killing of Mrs. Heinrichsen?"

"Yeah. It is. Did you know her?"

"No. I have heard of her, though. Sounds like a nasty old hag to me. Probably deserved what she got."

I cleared my throat. "I hardly think anyone deserves to be killed, no matter how horrible they have acted."

Stephan had taken a beer and was drinking from it. "I completely disagree."

"I beg your pardon? How does killing them make it better?"

"Who says it's supposed to make anything better? It's not. It's all about revenge, them getting what they deserve. I don't feel sorry for anyone like her."

"So, I guess you're into the death penalty and that kind of stuff?"

He drank from his beer and nodded. "I sure am. An eye for an eye, I always say. If someone kills a person, they should be killed themselves. It's as simple as that."

"Here's the water." Sophia lifted the pitcher and started pouring water into our small glasses.

I drank a little, thinking about saying something more, but I didn't want to ruin the atmosphere by starting an argument. The man had a right to his own opinion, even if I didn't agree with it.

"Now, dig in," Stephan said.

I picked up my knife and fork and cut out a piece of the meat. It tasted heavenly. The sauce with mushrooms in it was like an explosion in my mouth.

"Wow, this is good," Sophia said. "What is it? I can't tell what kind of meat it is?"

Stephan lifted his head and smiled. "It's actually two types of meat. A real delicacy. It's heart and liver in a creamy mushroom sauce."

Sophia had just taken a big mouthful and now she was spitting it all out on the plate. I felt the meat grow in my mouth and chewed for a long time until I finally sank it with much discomfort. I flushed it down with a big sip of wine.

"Are you kidding me?" Sophia yelled and washed her mouth out with water, gurgling and splashing it around inside her mouth like she was cleaning her teeth at the dentist.

"What?" Stephan said.

I poked my meat with my fork and pushed it around on the plate. I really didn't feel like eating any more.

"You served us organs?" Sophia asked, enraged.

"It's good. It's considered to be a delicacy. Didn't it taste good? Emma?" Stephan looked at me for an answer. It was starting to be awkward.

"It is great," I said. "I'm just not really into eating organs. My mother used to serve liver to me as a child, and I've kind of hated it ever since. Sorry."

Stephan threw his fork at his plate and pushed his chair backwards, making a loud sound. "Well, suit yourselves," he said in an angry tone.

"I'd better get back to my dad and the kids," I said and got up. I wiped my mouth on the napkin and emptied my wine. I sensed it was time to get out. Stephan wasn't happy with us and the atmosphere was way too tense for me to stay.

Sophia walked me out. "I'm so sorry about that," she whispered.

"It's okay. He didn't know. Thanks for dinner. See you soon," I gave her a hug before I left.

40

2012

I got up early and made breakfast for everyone. While frying bacon in the pan the way I knew my dad liked it, I couldn't help but think about last night and the food.

There was a sound behind me and I turned to see my dad walk into the kitchen wearing a bathrobe over his pajamas.

"Good morning, Dad," I said.

"What's with the cheerful voice this early?" he grunted and sat down heavily in a chair. I smiled and looked at him. He never was much of a morning person.

"I'm making bacon and scrambled eggs. Just the way you like them."

My dad picked up the local paper and started reading while grunting some more. I shrugged and continued my cooking, waiting for him to wake up properly. It always took a while.

"So, did you sleep alright?" I asked.

My dad grumbled. "I never slept well in this house, not one single night in my life."

"That's a little harsh, don't you think? Certainly there must have been nights in your childhood that you slept okay?"

My dad put the paper down and looked at me. "I hate this place, end of story. Just like I loathed my mother who died in it. I feel like she's still here watching me, condemning me. Hell, yesterday I even thought I heard her voice again. Telling me I was a fool for letting my wife run off like that." He shook his head with a tsk. "Sounded just like she used to. Always calling me a damned fool."

I flipped the bacon and turned to look at him again. "I don't think you're a fool. What could you have done? If Mom wanted to leave, she wanted to leave. It's not like you could have tied her up and made her stay."

My dad grunted again and folded the paper back up in front of his face. I approached him and sat down next to him. "Dad?"

"Hmm?"

"Dad, could you put the paper down, please?" I asked and put a hand on it.

He lowered it and looked at me over the edge.

"Just put it down for me, please. I like to look at people when I'm talking to them."

My dad grumbled some more, then put the paper down. He took off his glasses. "What do you want?"

"To know what went wrong with you and grandma. I grew up not knowing her at all. You even told me at one point she was already dead."

"You met her once."

"When I was four years old! If I wanted to get really angry, then I'd say you deprived me of a relationship with her by keeping me away."

My dad snorted. "Well you're better off without. Believe me. I did you a huge favor."

I sighed. "What's done is done and we can't change that, but I would like to know what went wrong with you two? Did you have a fight or what?"

My dad shook his head. "Can't we just leave it in the past? Do we have to talk about everything?"

"Dad. We hardly ever talk about anything important like this. I want to know because it will make me closer to you. It will make me understand you better and know you better. And I really want that."

"If you want to be so damn close, you shouldn't have moved all the way across the country now, should you?"

"Okay, Dad. I understand you're mad about us moving away and all..."

"Damn right I am. You're the only family I have left. Now, you're depriving me of a relationship with my grandchildren. Is that any better than what I did to you?"

"Touché, Dad. Okay, I admit I feel bad about having left you alone, and I promise we will come to visit as often as we can. And you can come here all the time of you like."

"Well, I don't like it. I don't like this island or this house."

"Why, Dad? What did grandma do that was so horrible it has to ruin everything for us? Explain it to me. Make me understand."

My dad scoffed. "Some things are better left in the past." He picked up the paper again while I watched him, feeling my irritation grow. This was so typical of him. I took a loud breath. My dad lowered the paper again.

"What?" he said. "You don't have to know everything."

"What are you so afraid of?" I asked with a scoff. "That I'll get to know you better? Is that so bad? It's just like when Mom left. You didn't even tell me about it. I called you the day after and you didn't even care to tell me. The only way I figured it out was because I stopped by a week later. A week later!"

"Don't raise your voice, Emma," he said, sounding like he had when I was still a child. "I thought your mother would call you and tell you herself. That's why I didn't talk about it. Plus, I was still very angry and sad, and I was afraid I might say something that I would later regret. You could say I was still in some sort of shock. I had no idea it was coming. I thought we were doing fine. You have to understand, Emma, that it came out of the blue for me. I was in no way prepared for it; I was still trying to figure out what had really happened when you called me. I wasn't prepared to accept the fact that she had left yet. There you have it. That's the truth."

I put my hand on top of his and held it tight. "I know, Dad. I know it has been a hard time for you. It must have been terrible. Hell, I have no idea why she would suddenly do such a thing, believe me. But what really hurt me was the fact that you didn't think about talking to me about it right away. You should have called me as soon as she left. I'm your daughter, for crying out loud. I will always be there for you. I want to be a part of your life. I want to know when you're sad and unhappy and when you're happy. Just like you want to be a part of my life and know what's going on with me."

Dad nodded slowly. "I guess I never thought about it in that way. I thought I was protecting you by not telling you. I didn't want you to see me unhappy. Guess that comes with being a parent, right? I didn't want you to feel like you had to take care of me."

I got up from my chair and kissed Dad on the forehead. "Coffee?" I asked, and poured some in a cup, knowing how much he loved his morning caffeine. I put it on the table in front of him and poured a mug for myself, too. He lifted his and clinked against mine in a toast.

"I love you, kiddo," he said. "Even though you insist on living all the way out here."

"I love you, too, Dad."

I served him his breakfast and he tore into the bacon and eggs with great pleasure. "What about work?" I asked, knowing how important Dad's work as a doctor has always had been to him. In fact, so much so that he had been absent a lot during my childhood and during his marriage to my mother, something I assumed had a lot to say in her decision to leave him.

"Aren't they going to miss you at the clinic this entire week?"

"I took the week off. It's my clinic, you know. I can take time off if I want to. Plus, I just hired a new guy, so there are three physicians to take care of patients from now on. I was thinking I might even take a lot more time off, since they seem to run the place just fine without me. Maybe even better." My dad winked as he said the last sentence.

"That sounds like a very good idea," I said, thinking that I never expected I would hear my dad say something like that, ever.

"Yeah, I guess. I have kind of wasted most of my life at that clinic, huh? Missed most of the years you were growing up. If only I had realized this many years ago, I might even still have a wife."

I smiled compassionately, knowing he might be right. "Well, Dad, as you put it yourself, some things are better left in the past, right? We don't have time to waste on regrets."

He nodded, taking a sip of his coffee. "You're right. I'm trying to look ahead now and my future is with my family. It's with you and the two young ones."

I twisted the edge of my napkin, shredding it a little. "Not as young as they used to be anymore. The oldest one seems to think she doesn't need any of us anymore."

"Oh, but she does. Believe me. She needs you more than ever."

I nodded. "You're probably right."

We sat in silence for a couple of heartbeats. Then he looked at me and spoke:

"If you must know, it wasn't an argument that went wrong between your grandmother and me."

"Then what was it?"

"She could be a very controlling woman. She wanted to control my life, tell me what to do and who to do it with. I had to break out of her grip; I had to turn my back on her if I wanted a life of my own. Otherwise, I would be living her life and not mine. You need to let your kids make their own mistakes. You can't always keep them within your control just because you want to protect them."

"She wanted you to be one of those church people?" I asked, and ate some scrambled egg. It tasted bland. I put some salt on it and kept eating.

"Yes. Among other things. I didn't like it there and wanted out. I wanted to get away from all this, all these people, away from the church and the island, but she wouldn't let me. That was one of the major things. She wanted to rule my life. So, one night, I just left.

Packed my things and left the house. Took the morning ferry out of here. I called her when I had reached the mainland and she told me that if I didn't come back right away, she would disown me. I was no longer her son and shouldn't bother coming back. She could be very angry at times and very irrational. I do believe she regretted having been that harsh to me later in her life, but she never told me. Well, she let me inherit the money after all, so maybe that was her way of telling me."

"What else?"

"She wanted me to marry one of the girls from the church. A good Christian girl, as she put it. I told her I didn't want to. She never approved of your mother. She wasn't good enough for me, she kept telling me." My dad scoffed. "And look at me now. Maybe she was right, huh?"

"At least it was your choice to make. Plus, you had some good years with Mom."

"And we had you," he said.

I took a bite of the eggs, and then washed them down with some orange juice. I wanted to ask him about grandmother being killed in this house and what he knew, but was interrupted when suddenly I saw something out of my kitchen window—or rather, someone. I got up and walked towards it to get a better look.

"What's up?" my dad asked.

"What's he doing out on the street on his own?" I mumbled.

"Who's out on the street alone?"

"Johan. Sophia's youngest son. He's only two, he shouldn't be running around in the street all by himself, playing without adult supervision."

"Who would let a two-year-old play unsupervised in the street?"

"Exactly. His mother certainly wouldn't. Something is very wrong." I grabbed my jacket from the closet in the hall and looked at my dad through the door. "Could you stay here for when Victor wakes up? I have a bad feeling about this."

"Sure."

41

2012

Johan was sitting on the asphalt in the middle of the road, playing with his small toy truck when I got out to him.

"Johan? Buddy? What are you doing out here on your own?" I grabbed him and lifted him up in my arms. He continued playing with his truck, making sounds with his mouth. His diaper was heavy, like it hadn't been changed this morning at all. It worried me. Sophia had a lot of kids and got overwhelmed sometimes, but I had never ever seen her leave a dirty diaper on any of her kids. This was wrong. This was very wrong.

Feeling the anxiety grow inside of me, I walked quickly towards Sophia's house, carrying Johan. My heart started beating faster when I saw that the front door was ajar. I pushed it open and found the rest of Sophia's kids running around, screaming, yelling, and crying in the kitchen and living room. The house was an extreme mess.

"Sophia?" I yelled.

I tried to shush the kids to hear if she was answering me, maybe from the shower or something, but there was nothing.

Had she left them? Maybe to go get something? No, she would never. Sophia would never leave her kids home alone.

I found the oldest, Christoffer, who was seven like my Victor, and grabbed him by the shoulder. "Where is your mother?" I asked.

He shrugged. "I don't know."

"When did you last see her?"

"Last night?" he said.

"Last night! Didn't you see her this morning?"

He shook his head.

"Have you checked her bedroom?"

"Yes. She wasn't there."

I let go of Christoffer and stormed into the bedroom. The bed was untouched. I gasped and called out for her again and again. "Sophia! Where are you?"

But, no answer. The kids were all crying now and Christoffer stood in the doorway looking abandoned. I kneeled in front of him. "We'll find her Christoffer. Don't you worry, okay? She has to be here somewhere, right?" I tried to sound convincing, but didn't think I was. Underneath my shirt, my heart was beating so fast it almost hurt.

"Mommy!" one of the kids suddenly said. A little girl named Ida. She had snot running from her nose and tears in her eyes. She was in one of the children's rooms and pointing out the window facing the yard. I rushed towards it and looked out.

There, in the middle of the high grass, lay Sophia. I gasped and turned to look at the children, whom were all staring at me like they were expecting me to magically make their mother appear in here. Ida was crying and hammering on the window.

"Mommy?"

I pulled her away and shut the curtains. "You, Christoffer. You take care of your siblings now, all right? I have to go into the yard. Make sure they stay in here. Put on a video or something."

Christoffer was tearing up; He rubbed his eyes and nodded.

"I'll be right back, okay?"

Then I ran outside. *Oh, no. Oh, God, no. Please let her be alive. Please let her be alive.*

As I came closer, I realized she wasn't moving. She was lying still in the grass. Naked. Her body was bruised. I fought my tears as I came closer and kneeled next to her. Her face was so badly beaten I could hardly recognize her. It was all swollen and purple.

"Please be alive; please be sleeping."

I leaned down and listened to her breath and put a finger on her throat to feel her pulse. It was there. It was weak, but she was still alive.

Thank God!

"Sophia?" I said. It was hard to keep the tears away. "Sophia? What happened to you?"

Sophia opened her badly bruised eyes. "Are you awake, Sophia?" I cried. "Please, wake up!"

Sophia's body jerked and she bent over and threw up on the ground.

"Oh, God, Sophia, what the hell happened to you. Who did this to you?"

Sophia spat and blood landed in the grass. She felt her cracked lip and had blood on her fingers. I helped her get up. She held on to me as we walked towards the house.

"Do you want me to take you to the hospital?" I asked.

Sophia lifted her hand. "No," she said. "No hospital. No police."

"Why? Whoever did this has to pay."

She shook her head while we walked. Tears were rolling fast across my cheeks.

"I did this," she said. I could tell it hurt for her to talk. "I did this to myself."

Anger rose in me. "No. That's a lie and you know it!"

"Just help me get inside, will you? I need a shower. I don't want my kids to see me like this. Could you help me keep them away until I'm in the shower?"

I nodded, feeling helpless. I had to respect her wishes, even though I didn't agree with her about not reporting it to the police. I also really wanted her to go to the emergency room to be checked. But I couldn't force her.

"Of course."

42

2012

I told the kids to keep watching the movie in the bedroom and that their mother was just in the shower and would be out in a few moments.

When Sophia got out, she didn't look much better than she had outside.

"That bad, huh?" she asked when she saw my reaction.

I shook my head. "Worse. Don't you think we should have a doctor look at you?"

She shook her head.

"What about the baby? We need to make sure it's all right? We need to be sure that you're all right," I argued.

Sophia coughed. I could tell it hurt. "Well, I'm not, am I? I'm not okay."

"Let me at least help you into bed. You need rest."

Sophia tried to nod, but it was too painful. I helped her into her bedroom, then put her under her covers. I went to the kitchen and made her some soup from a can, then fed her with a spoon.

"So, are you ever going to tell me who did this to you?" I asked.

Sophia sighed deeply and turned her head away.

"It was Stephan, right?"

She didn't have to answer. The fact that she didn't protest told me all I needed to know.

Sophia's eyes welled up. I gave her another spoonful of soup. She was crying. "I thought he was a good one, Emma. I really did."

"I know, sweetie. He seemed really nice, too." I stroked her hair gently, avoiding the bruises on her forehead.

Sophia scoffed. "It was the thing with the food that ticked him off. Because we didn't want to eat his food. He got so mad, Emma. I don't think I've ever seen anyone explode like that. He was yelling and screaming at me. I thought he would wake up the kids, so I told him to take it outside. Then he hit me with something hard and dragged me outside, pulled me by the hair. I don't know much about what happened after that. But I do remember it hurt when he kicked me." She tried to look at me. "Do you think the baby is alright?"

"I don't know, sweetie. I honestly don't know. You need someone to take a look at you. You really do." I was trying hard not to cry, but I failed miserably.

"It's embarrassing, Emma. You know how they talk on this island. If I call Dr. Williamsen, everybody will know what happened. His secretary, Lise will make sure to tell. She never was able to keep quiet about anything. I just can't face that right now. I don't want my kids to be the trash of town, if you know what I mean?"

"My dad is a doctor. Will you let him take a look at you? I promise he won't talk about it to anyone. He's an outsider. He grew up here and knows how it all works and hates it more than anyone. Please? I'll tell him to keep it quiet."

Sophia closed her eyes and leaned her head back on the pillow. "All right, then."

Five minutes later, I had my entire family at Sophia's house. Maya and Victor stayed with the kids and Maya tried to take care of all of them, while Dad examined Sophia. I waited outside the door, and as soon as he opened it I looked at him, waiting for answers.

"It's bad," he said. "She's really badly beaten up. Who did this to her? Some boyfriend?"

"Yes. What about the baby? Is the baby okay?"

My dad sighed and nodded. "I think it'll be fine. It's still too early to say for sure, but I am optimistic. I'll check in on her tomorrow, so it's good I was planning on staying, huh?"

"You are a lifesaver. You have no idea, Dad. This means the world to me. Thank you."

"You're welcome, kiddo. Make sure she stays in bed and that she's careful in the coming days. She suffered a severe trauma to her head and she needs rest. All the rest she can get."

I nodded. "We'll have to help her with that."

"I guess we all need to get to work, then," Dad said. "I'll help you."

"Me too." I heard something, turned my head and saw Maya standing behind me. "How long have you been standing there?"

"Long enough. I'm old enough to understand more than you think. I'd like to help Sophia out. Besides, next week is fall break, so I don't have school. I'll take care of her kids with you."

I felt a pinch in my heart. I leaned over and kissed my daughter, suddenly realizing she had become taller than me. I looked at her proudly.

"Let's get those kids over to our house," I said. "Lord knows we have enough room for all of them."

"What about Victor?" Maya asked. "He doesn't do well with many people around."

"Don't worry about Victor. I'll take care of him," I said.

43

1985

Sebastian was crying. Ever since his mother died, he had felt so lonely. Her body was still on the bed, where she had last looked at him, last spoken to him, last touched him. He picked up her cold hand and put it against his cheek, pretending that she was stroking him like she used to.

Then he called her name. "Mommy? Please wake up. Please talk to me."

Her lifeless body looked strange and somehow these small flies had suddenly found their way into the shelter and were swarming her. Sebastian felt so alone, so abandoned, and so scared. He knew about death. His mother had told him about it, but he didn't know that it looked like this.

Sebastian let go of his mother's hand and turned to watch his spiders. They were crawling around on the walls of the shelter. He grabbed one of them and played with it in his hand. He let it crawl up his arm and up till it reached his throat. He picked up another one and played with it in his hand. He glanced at his mother. He didn't like to look at her anymore, her face, yes, but not her legs.

I'm so sorry, Mommy. You know I'm sorry, don't you?

Sebastian crept up in his own bed and continued to play with his spider when suddenly he heard something. A sound coming from...*Oh, God, could it really be?* There it was again. Another sound. Coming from the other side of the door. The outside that he had never seen, but only heard and read of in the books the lady had brought him. Could it be her? Was she finally bringing him food?

Sebastian jumped up from the bed and walked towards the iron door. He heard a rattle and a clatter just like they used to hear when the lady came with the food. It had to be her. It just had to be. Sebastian prepared himself for seeing her and telling her what had happened to his mother.

Will she understand? Will she blame me?

Another rattle and the lock was unlocked. Sebastian knew this sound and was filled with hope and joy. Finally, someone came. Finally, he wasn't alone anymore. She hadn't forgotten about them. The lady still remembered.

The lock was removed and the door opened carefully. What appeared once it had opened entirely shocked Sebastian in a way he would never forget. It wasn't the old lady that stuck her head in like she used to. No, this was something else. It was a small girl. Her hair was braided on each side and she was wearing a purple dress. Sebastian had never seen such a beautiful creature before except in his books, and he kept staring at her. She smiled and waved at him. Then she spoke:

"Hi."

Sebastian swallowed hard. He didn't know if he was supposed to answer. He didn't know if she was dangerous. The girl kept looking around like she had never seen such a place before in her life. There was something about her, something intriguing, something alluring, and Sebastian felt all kinds of emotions he had never experienced before.

"Who are you?" she asked.

Sebastian stood up straight, thinking that in case she turned out to be dangerous, he wanted to make sure she knew he wasn't going to give up without a fight.

"S-S-Sebastian," he stuttered.

She waved again with a smile. "Hi, Sebastian. You know you have a spider on your face, right?"

Sebastian felt his cheek and the spider climbed back on his hand. He looked at the girl, then reached out the hand with the spider on it to hand it to her.

The little girl didn't seem as thrilled as he was with the small creature. She wrinkled her nose, then let out a scream. It startled Sebastian and he pulled his hand away. He looked behind her and spotted light coming from the open door behind her. The second door that his mother had talked about. The one leading out to the... leading *outside*.

The girl kept looking at him. "Do you want to play?" she asked.

That was when Sebastian remembered what his mother had once told him.

If the door opens and you have the chance, you run. Do you hear me? You run, Sebastian. Run all you can, don't let anyone stop you. And don't talk to anyone, don't tell them who you are or where you're from. Do you promise me that, son?

Yes, Mommy.

"Yes, Mommy," he repeated now, standing in front of the girl.

"What?" she asked, but Sebastian didn't hear her. The alluring light coming from the big outside pulled him forward, as he sprang towards the girl and pushed her aside. She let out a small shriek as she fell to the side and Sebastian sprang for the door. He pushed it all the way up and was blinded by the strong sunlight that he had never seen before. But he was able to see enough to run. So he did; Sebastian sprinted across the yard and behind him he heard a male voice calling:

"Emma? Emmaaa? Your grandmother is coming back from the hospital now. Her car is pulling up now. Where are you, Emma?"

44

2012

I'm standing in front of a boy. I have never seen him before. He has a spider on his face. I'm asking him to play with me. I'm four years old and visiting my grandmother for the first and last time in my life. The boy doesn't want to play with me. He runs away. My dad is calling. I go back to the house and get ready to greet my grandmother. I tell him I saw a boy in the yard. He tells me to not make up stories. My grandmother's car is driving up into the driveway. She has been in the hospital for three weeks. Broken hip and she needed a replacement. She gets out of the car and walks up towards me leaning on her crutches. I am looking forward to talking to her; after all, she is family, my grandmother, my dad's mother. She must be happy to finally see me, but she's not. She is angry. She yells at my dad. I feel angry, I yell at her to be nicer to my dad, and then she turns and yells at me. She calls me a brat.

"We never should have come," my dad says and pulls my arm. "Nothing has changed."

. . .

I woke up bathed in sweat. It was morning, but still early. None of the kids were awake. I was panting heavily.

It was just a dream, I told myself. But I knew it had happened. I'd had this dream over and over throughout my childhood. Suddenly, I remembered. Suddenly, I recognized it.

"The boy," I said. "There was a boy."

I jumped out of bed and went into my closet. I pulled out a big flashlight. I put on a bathrobe and started walking downstairs.

I had found the key. How had I found the key? The way most curious four-year-olds find almost anything, especially when they know they're not allowed to.

I remembered how the key had felt in my hand as a child. Now, I walked to the hallway downstairs, found the old armoire, and pulled out the drawer. I gasped. It was still there. Reaching in, I grabbed it in my hand. My heart was pounding as I looked at it under the glow of the flashlight.

How did I know? How did I know what it was for?

I remembered how I had tried it on all kinds of locks in the house. The strange house I was visiting with my dad. I remembered how it made him grumpy just to be here. I never understood why.

I found the hatch first, then I tried the key on it. I didn't know it would fit. I was playing explorer and wanted to see what was down there. Oh, my God. I tripped over the hatch just like Victor did, and then I decided to try the key to see if it would fit.

I walked through the living room and out into the yard. The trees looked big and creepy in the darkness. The sun hadn't risen yet, but it wasn't going to be long before it did. I walked with determined steps in between the trees, still picturing the boy with the spider on his face.

I found the hatch and wiped away leaves to find the lock. It was rusty and old. I put the key in and turned. It opened. The door was heavy, so I had to use both hands to pull it open. A couple of stairs appeared and at the end of them was another iron door with a lock. I walked down and put the key in just like I had done back then. It opened immediately. I pulled the door open and peeked in. In a quick glimpse I thought I saw the boy again, standing in the opening with his pale face, glaring at me like I was the strangest thing he had ever seen.

I sniffled and breathed heavily. I didn't understand. What was that boy doing down there? Why was he in this old bunker all by himself? And why was the door locked?

I didn't like to think about it. I lifted up the flashlight and let its light fall inside of the bunker. Two beds, nicely made, lots of empty shelves, blankets, pillows, books and old magazines on some of them. I lit up the walls and gasped. They were plastered in drawings. Time had turned the paper brown and dirty. I stepped inside and lit them all up with my flashlight. Hundreds of drawings made by a child. Drawings of a little boy and his mother sailing on a boat, drawings of a little boy and his mother on top of a mountain. I stared at all the many drawings, wondering who made them and why they were in here.

A spider climbed up the wall and startled me. I stared at it for a long time. I felt tears roll across my cheeks and wiped them away. What was all this? I didn't understand. I didn't *want* to understand.

45

1985

Old Mrs. Frost read about the boy in the paper. Someone had found him on the ferry headed towards the mainland. How he had managed to sneak on board, nobody knew, and now they didn't know where he came from or whom he belonged to, and they were asking people for help. A big picture covered the front page, but Mrs. Frost didn't need any picture to recognize him. She folded the paper so the picture was hidden and looked out the window into the yard where the boy and his mother had lived for so long.

After coming back from the hospital with a new hip, Mrs. Frost had walked down to the bunker at the end of the yard on her crutches. She could tell the door was open from afar and knew it was bad. The bunker turned out to be empty. The boy was gone. With much difficulty, she climbed inside.

Damn these old bones that she should fall and break her hip right then when they needed new supplies. Mrs. Frost had cursed every day she needed to stay at the hospital, and to be frank, she thought she would come back only to find both of them had starved to death. But, somehow, the boy had survived.

She walked down the many stairs and walked inside, groaning

and moaning, and there, inside on one of the beds was her answer to how the boy had managed to stay alive.

She walked closer, humping on her crutches, trying to put as little weight on her new hips as possible. The stench from the dead body was horrendous. Mrs. Frost found a handkerchief in her pocket and held it in front of her nose as she examined the body and especially the lower parts of it.

Half of the meat on one side of her stomach was missing, and so was most on the right side of her leg. Now it was covered in flies and ants. Mrs. Frost shook her head in disbelief. As she walked back to the house, humping on her crutches, she mumbled under her breath.

"You little bastard. You ate her, didn't you? You ate your own mother to survive."

Now she was staring at his picture in the paper and she got the feeling he was somehow staring back at her. The article stated that he hadn't spoken a word so far, so they didn't even know if he was Danish or maybe a German tourist who had somehow gotten away from his parents.

"So, you've decided to keep quiet, huh?" she said to the picture. "Well, you're smart, my boy. Very smart."

Mrs. Frost picked up the phone on the end table next to the chair she was sitting in and dialed a number.

"Mrs. Heinrichsen. Have you seen the paper? No. No. I don't think he will pose any problem for us. After all, he is just a young boy. What can he do? Yes. I'll make sure to notify the pastor as well. Do you think we need to speak to Irene Justesen, too, tell her he is on the loose? No, no. You're right. She doesn't need to know. She's so busy with all that fitness mumbo-jumbo. She is no longer one of us. There's the risk that she'll try and find him or something and then it will all blow up in our faces. I believe in keeping a low profile. He won't say anything if we don't, I'm sure. Goodnight Mrs. Heinrichsen and God bless."

Mrs. Frost hung up the phone, suddenly feeling uncomfortable in her own living room with all those big black windows. She got up and leaned on her crutches. She pulled the curtains to cover all the windows to stop the eerie feeling of someone watching her from the outside. As she grabbed one of the curtains, a spider jumped right at her face and landed in her hair. Mrs. Frost screamed and let go of her crutches, falling to the ground with a loud crash and hurting her leg.

Lying on the floor, she moaned for someone to please help her, please help an old lady. But there was no one but her and the spider left in the big old house.

46

2012

I ran into my dad's bedroom and woke him up.

"What's going on, sweetie? Is it something with Sophia? Is she not feeling well?"

"No. No. It's not her." I was gasping for air after having run across the yard, up the stairs, and into his room.

"Is it one of the kids?"

I shook my head. "No. No. That's not it either." I felt my eyes tearing up and couldn't hold it back any longer. My dad saw it and wiped a tear away with his thumb.

"What's the matter then, honey?"

"Do you remember when we came to visit Grandma while she was at the hospital when I was only four years old?"

My dad rubbed his eyes. "Vaguely, why?"

"Do you remember I was in the yard when you called for me, when Grandma came back and we all ended up yelling at each other?"

"No. I do remember her yelling at you, though. That's when I decided we had to leave again. We had been staying at the house for several days, cleaning and making sure it was ready for her when she got back. I remember I was angry that she wasn't the least bit grateful for what we had done. We left right away and that was actually the last time I saw her alive."

"There was a boy," I said and sniffed, trying to hold back the tears. "Do you remember? I told you there was a boy? Right before Grandma came home."

"You have a very detailed memory of that day all of a sudden, don't you? No, I don't remember that there was a boy or that you said that."

"I dreamt about it. I thought it was just a dream, but it wasn't. It was real. There is a hatch that leads to a hole, a room underground in the yard."

"The old bunker, yes."

"Have you ever been down there?"

"No. My mom kept it locked up. But I do know that she kept it ready in case war broke out again. She did grow up during World War II, you know. Always afraid it was going to happen again. She never forgave the Germans."

"There was a boy inside the shelter that day. I found the key by coincidence a couple of days before and then I tripped over the hatch and found it was locked. I went back to get the key and it fit. When I unlocked it and opened it, there he was. Looking back at me. What was he doing down there, Dad?"

My dad shook his head. "I have no idea what you're talking about. Are you sure you're all right, dear? Maybe you just had a very lively dream or something? Do you have a fever?"

"I'm not sick, Dad. I'm not sleeping either. I'm very much awake. I don't think I've ever been this awake before in my life. I need to know what that boy was doing down there, Dad. Why was he locked inside of the bunker in the ground?" I was almost yelling now and my dad looked at me, frightened.

"What's going on here?" he asked. "I don't understand anything of what you're saying."

I shrugged and turned away. "Neither do I. But I have a bad

feeling about this, Dad. I went down there again. I went into the bunker."

"Now? At this time at night?"

"It's six in the morning. It's hardly night anymore. The kids will be waking up soon, anyway. And, yes, I went back into the bunker. I found the key in the same place and went in there. And guess what I found?"

My dad sighed and rubbed his face. "I don't know? Another little boy?"

"Drawings, Dad. The walls are plastered with drawings made by a child. Old drawings like they were made a long time ago."

"I really don't know what to say to all this," my dad said and leaned back on his pillow.

"Do you think your mother kept the boy down there for some reason? Do you think she had locked him down there?"

"No," he chuckled. "My mother was many things, among them bad tempered and controlling, but I refuse to believe she could be that cruel."

47

2012

The man was looking down at the pot and he inhaled the wonderful scent coming from it. He added some more bouillon and rosemary. It had been cooking since seven this morning, but that's the way he preferred it. Letting it simmer for hours and hours softened the meat and made it very tasty.

He was planning an early dinner for himself, since he was going to have a busy night. The heart was what needed the longest cooking, so he had put that in first. Now he found his knife and threw a big lump of meat up on the table. He started cutting the lungs into smaller edible pieces before he put them into the pot, too. Lastly, there was the liver. He took it out of the refrigerator and threw it on the table that was covered in blood from all of the chopping and preparing. He lifted his knife up high and closed his eyes as the blade went through the meat and produced the most intoxicating sound to him. He cut it into slices that all ended up in the pot, along with the rest of the meat. Then some thyme and more rosemary. Now all it needed was time.

"A good nice meal, strong on proteins," he said, and put the lid back on. Then he turned the heat down.

It was a little after lunch, but he still felt he deserved a glass of red wine, so he opened a bottle, poured some in the pot and drank some of it from the bottle.

"It's five o'clock somewhere," he said to himself, looking at his reflection in the mirror on his wall. His skin was still pale and never did cope well with much sunlight. Even after all these years. You could still see all of his veins through his skin. It didn't matter. Made him kind of special, he thought. Unique. And he was one of a kind. He knew that much.

They had given him a new name. After finding him on the ferry, the police and social workers had tried everything to make him speak. But after weeks of silence and no one turning up to claim him, they didn't know what to do with him. So they sent him to an orphanage, where he was given a new name. For years, he still didn't speak, not until he was much older, and by then, they had stopped asking questions.

But he never forgot the name his mother had given him in the bunker where he was born, and when he was alone, he sometimes called himself his real name.

"Sebastian," he said it out loud now, watching himself in the mirror.

He had liked that name, but he had never liked that boy that he used to be. He was buried in the bunker along with his mother. With the new name came a new life. Sebastian got an education, and once done with high school, he got to finally see the world. He worked as a waiter in a restaurant, where he picked up a lot of his cooking skills, then he saved a lot of money and finally travelled around the world with nothing but his backpack. Sebastian enjoyed the great plains. He climbed mountains, slept under the endless starry sky, surfed waves in the ocean, and all the time he thought about how much his mother would have loved this. How she would have liked to be there with him under the open sky with no walls to keep her.

Once he came back, he started planning her revenge. He wanted those people that had done those bad things to his mother to suffer.

He moved back to the island and began a new life for himself, got close to the people, and it didn't take him long to find out exactly who he needed to punish. Who had been behind it all. He knew about Mrs. Frost, that she had locked his mother in there while she was pregnant because she didn't want her son to have to marry her, because it was a scandal that the girl had gotten pregnant outside of marriage when she was only sixteen. On top of that, he knew that the girl wasn't very bright and especially not suitable for her only son, heir to her fortune. He knew all about that even before he came back. His mom had told him those things while they were still down there. She had told him the truth. The rest he figured out on his own. He got close to them, they trusted him, and now...now there was only the last one left.

"Always save the best for last," he said, as he found his set of knives and started sharpening them. "Mother always said: Save the best for last."

48

2012

My dad and I went to check on Sophia right after breakfast. Maya promised to look after all the kids while we were gone.

"Are you sure you can do that?" I asked and looked at my beautiful daughter, whose strength in this time of crisis had impressed me. "Five kids...and Victor. It's a lot of hard work."

"Of course I can," she said, and kneeled in front of Sophia's youngest son, who was sitting on the floor with two wooden spoons and a pot that Maya had taken from the kitchen, and now he was playing it like it was a drum. I smiled and blew her a kiss. I think I was the proudest mother in the world at that instant. Seeing my daughter stand up like that had touched my heart.

"We'll be right back. Victor told me he'll stay in his room. I think all these kids kind of get to him, but he'll be fine as long as he stays up there."

I followed my dad across the street and into Sophia's house, where he went into the bedroom alone first. I heard him talk to her and then she answered. She sounded more like herself than she had the day before. It was a relief.

I waited for ten minutes or so until my dad came out of the room.

"How is she?" I asked.

"Better. Definitely improving. But she needs her rest. She should stay in bed for at least a couple of days more. At least," my dad said.

"I'll make sure the kids stay at our place till she's ready. Can I see her?"

"Sure. She was just asking for you. Go right in. I'll head back to assist Maya with all the munchkins before they eat her alive."

I smiled and watched my dad's face. He looked like he was enjoying this.

"See you over there in a bit, then," I said, and knocked on the door to Sophia's bedroom.

"Come in," Sophia said.

I opened the door and went in. Her face was still unrecognizable, and all of a sudden I felt really glad that her kids were at my house and that they didn't have to see their mother like this.

"How are my kids? They aren't too much trouble, are they?"

I shook my head and grabbed a chair. I pulled it close to her bed and sat down. "No, they have been very sweet. Maya is playing with them now and my dad just went back there to help her out."

"And you're fine with it? I mean...it kind of ruins your dad's visit and all."

"Stop worrying about stuff like that. I don't mind having them. You have to focus on getting well. The kids love our place and we love having them there."

Sophia tried to smile, but it was too hard. I grabbed her hand and held it in mine. Tears kept pressing, but I withheld them. "So, how are you feeling today?"

A tear escaped from her swollen eyes. "Why would he do this to me? I don't understand."

I held her hand tighter in mine and stroke it on top. "I don't know, Sophia."

"I keep thinking, if I only..."

I interrupted her. "No! Don't you even think that, Sophia. This guy is a maniac. He's a psychopath and you really should report him before he does this to anyone else. I think he is a very sick man, if you ask me."

"You think he might have done this before?" Sophia asked.

"Of course he has. He's a sick man, Sophia. He needs to be stopped. Let me talk to the police, let me tell them what happened, let them take him in for questioning. All you have to do is tell your story when they come to take your statement. I'll help you with the rest. I believe you're not only helping yourself, but all the other women he might run into in the future. A man like that needs to be locked up."

Sophia sniffled. I found a tissue and wiped her running nose. "Okay," she said. "You talk to them and report what he has done. But, promise me one thing."

I smiled and wiped her nose again. "Anything."

"Tell Officer Dan Toft. Let him handle everything. I trust him."

I nodded eagerly. "Of course. I'll make sure to talk to him."

49

2012

When I stepped out of Sophia's house, heavy grey clouds had gathered in the sky, making it almost pitch dark. I started walking when suddenly I heard my name being called.

"Emma?"

Someone was waving.

"Jack?" I said and walked closer. He ran towards me. He seemed unusually happy. He was wearing that beanie of his. For once, it was appropriate...with the cold wind. I smiled.

"What's up?"

"Is S-S-Sophia okay? I heard s-s-she was sick?"

"Well. Yes. It's a long story. It would be better if she told you herself, but we have the kids at our house for now. To give her rest."

"I-I-I was w-w-wondering if you would like to come over for dinner later in the afternoon? I was making an early dinner for myself, and foolish me, I have made way too much food."

I smiled again. There was nothing I'd rather do right at that moment. I really liked Jack and would like to get to know him better. Preferably to a point where he didn't stutter when he was near me. Like the afternoon I was at his house, when he had been relaxed and we had a really nice time together. "Thank you. That's so sweet of you. I would really like that. But I'm afraid I can't today. I have to do something for Sophia and I can't leave my dad and Maya alone with all those kids for that long. But maybe tomorrow?"

Jack seemed confused. He bit his lip. "B-B-But tomorrow the food w-w-will be no g-g-good."

"Then we'll make some new."

"I wanted so badly to show you my new p-p-picture." Jack's face was so disappointed I could hardly take it. I put my hand on his shoulder. "You know what? Maybe I'll come over for a little while later this afternoon. Right now, I have to go to town for a little bit, but when I get back I'll stop by and look at it, okay?"

Jack smiled again and suddenly reminded me of an older Victor. Maybe he was like him in some way. Maybe he had slight autism as well?

"That's a d-d-date, then," he said and started walking away.

"See you!" I yelled and walked to my own house. I found my dad and Maya in the living room playing with all five kids, who seemed to be having the time of their lives.

I signaled to my dad and he came closer.

"I need to go down to the police station," I said. "Sophia has agreed to report the bastard."

Dad gave me a warm hug. "That's great news. I didn't like thinking of him running around somewhere out there and hurting people."

I hugged him back. I had thought about Stephan a lot since I found Sophia in the yard. Something was really off with that guy and maybe it was more than just him enjoying beating the crap out of women. Maybe it was even deeper than that. Maybe...maybe he... Well, I couldn't help wondering about that food he had served for us.

What if Stephan had also killed people? What if he was the killer?

"Is it okay if I leave you all alone for a little while, then?" I asked.

My dad nodded. "Sure. No problem. I don't know about Maya and the kids, but I'm having a blast," he said. "But I don't know about

Victor. He doesn't seem to be taking this all too well. Maybe you should check on him before you leave. He's been in his room all morning, and when I checked on him last, he was sitting on his bed with his hands pressed against his ears. I tried to talk to him, but he didn't respond."

"He never liked loud noises too much, especially not the ones young children make. How he ever gets through an entire day in school is beyond me," I said. "I'll check in on him."

"Great," Dad said, and put on a cowboy hat. "Now, if you'll excuse me, I believe there's a need for a new sheriff in town." Then he pretended to ride an imaginary horse. I watched him ride off into the sunset before I ran up the stairs and knocked on the door to Victor's room.

He didn't answer, so I walked right in. He was still sitting like my dad had described him. In the middle of the bed, his legs pulled up under him and with both hands covering his ears. I approached him, and as he saw me, he let his hands come down.

"Mom. Can't you get those kids out of the house? They scream all the time. I can't stand it!"

I looked at him and tilted my head slightly. "That bad, huh?"

"Worse. It's terrible."

"All right. What do you say to coming out with me for a small drive? I'm going to the police station; maybe you'd like to come along?"

Victor's shoulders seemed to relax. "Please. Yes. Take me away from here."

"You know they're having a lot of fun in the living room, don't you?" I asked him, as we walked down the stairs together. "That's why they are yelling and screaming. They're just playing. You're missing out. Wouldn't you rather stay and play than go with me to a boring police station?"

Victor took one look into the living room, where my dad now was rolling on the floor with four kids on top of him, who were trying to ride him as a horse. I had to hold back my laughter. I had never seen my dad quite like this before. When I was a child, he was always too adult, too busy to play with me, and even when Victor and Maya were born, he had his clinic to take care of, and there was always some patient who needed him. It was like he had completely changed now. Maybe my mom leaving him wasn't such a bad thing, after all?

"No," Victor said, putting his hands over his ears again. "I want to go with you."

"It'll be very boring, Vic. Don't say I didn't warn you." I grabbed my long coat and told him to put on his short one.

When we walked out of the house, it had started to snow. I reached out my hand and grabbed a couple of flakes. "Now, what do you know? Snow in October? That's a first. What do you say, buddy?"

Victor shrugged.

"Ah, that's right," I said. "You already knew it was coming."

50

2012

The snow was coming down heavily as we drove across town towards the police station. The winds had picked up, too; I could tell by the trees surrounding the police station. I stopped the car at the small parking place outside the building, and then looked at Victor in the rearview mirror.

"It's snowing heavily now, buddy. Are you ready to run inside?"

He nodded without looking at me. He hadn't uttered a word the whole way down there. I figured he was enjoying the silence.

"Okay. Let's go."

I opened the door and got out. My hair was soaking wet before Victor had even gotten out of the car. We ran side by side towards the front door. Inside, two officers were at work. They seemed to be stressed and busy, constantly talking on the phone. I scanned the room, but didn't see Officer Dan anywhere. When one of the officers hung up, I approached the counter.

"Excuse me? Could you help me, please?"

"Yes, of course," the officer said. "I'm so sorry but this blizzard has taken us all by surprise. It wasn't foreseen by any of the meteorologists. Now we have a lot of citizens who need our help. Especially old people falling, and some are even stuck with their cars. It's really coming down hard out there, huh?"

"It sure is," I said.

"At this time of year," he said, looking surprised. "Don't think that ever happened before. So...what can I do for the two of you?"

"We were looking for Officer Dan Toft. Is he here somewhere?" I asked and looked behind him.

"Officer Dan usually has the night shift. He won't be in for another couple of hours. Is it something I can help with?"

I bit my lip. It would be easiest to just have this officer take the report and take care of everything, but I had made a promise to Sophia. I shook my head. "No. I'm afraid it has to be him. I'm sorry."

The officer shrugged. "Well, I guess we are kind of overwhelmed anyway right now, so if it can wait, then maybe it would be for the best."

I nodded while walking towards the front door. "Thanks anyway."

Back in the car, I hit my hand onto the wheel. "Crap!" I really wanted to get this done today, so they could have that guy put away. I didn't like that he was out there somewhere on the island, posing a threat to everybody. What if he had killed all those people? Maybe it was even one of his victim's heart and liver he was serving us that day? The thought made me nauseous. I started the car and backed out through a big pile of snow. Out on the road, the car was sliding from side to side, so I drove as slowly as possible while trying to see out through the front window.

"Snow in October," I mumbled.

"So, are we going back home already?" Victor asked.

I looked at him in the mirror. It had been my original plan, but now I wasn't so sure anymore. "You know what? What do you say we make one more stop on the way?"

Victor seemed relieved at the suggestion.

I turned right and let the car slide down another road. I remembered that Sophia had once told me that Officer Dan lived on one of the main streets downtown in a small red house on the corner of Poppelvej and Pilevej. It shouldn't be too hard to find.

I was right. A few minutes later, I parked the car in front of his house and got out. Victor followed me closely.

"Who lives here again?" he asked.

"A nice police officer who is going to help me out with something. His name is Dan."

51

2012

"**E**mma!"

Officer Dan seemed very happy to see me. He was looking very handsome, as always. "What can I do for you?" he asked.

"Can I come in? There's something I need to talk to you about."

Dan looked slightly confused, but opened the door and let Victor and me inside. "This is my son, Victor, by the way," I said.

Victor stormed past him without looking up.

"I'm sorry about that," I said. "He doesn't like strangers. It takes him a while."

Officer Dan closed the door behind me. "No problem at all. He is smart not to talk to any stranger in the street. You never know what their intentions are."

Victor found a couch and sat on it with his arms crossed in front of his chest.

"Is there somewhere we can go where he can't hear what we're saying?" I asked discretely.

"Sure. In the kitchen."

"Let's go in there."

"So, what can I do for you?" Officer Dan asked, motioning me to sit in one of the chairs around the small table. "Did you know you get a small wrinkle on your nose when you're upset?" His eyes gleamed as I felt my nose, then blushed.

"Do you want something to drink?" he asked. "I can't believe you went through that awful storm to get here. Do you want a beer? Or maybe a glass of wine?"

"I'm driving, remember?" I said.

"Of course. Sorry about that. Can I offer you a soda?"

"Sure."

Dan found an orange soda and opened it for me. He placed it in front of me on the table, and then he opened the door leading to the living room. "Do you think he would like one too?"

"Sure. Give him a Coke. That'll make his day. I never allow him to have that. You know the caffeine and all that sugar. Goes right into his blood."

Dan found a Coke and went into the other room to give it to Victor. Then the officer sat down in front of me. "Think I just made a new friend," he said.

"That was fast. It usually takes Victor weeks to change his mind."

"I gave him a bag of gummy bears, as well," Dan said and winked.

"Smart move."

"So, what can I do for you, Emma?"

"It's about Sophia, who lives on my street."

"I know her, yes. What's up with her?"

"She's been beaten up. Badly."

I saw Officer Dan's expression change drastically. "Why? Who would do such a thing?"

"I'm afraid it was her boyfriend. Stephan Olsen. He works as a chef at that place down by the harbor."

"Kabyssen?"

"That's it, yes. I found her in her yard yesterday. My dad's been checking up on her. He's a doctor. He says she's all right, but it's really bad. I convinced her to report it, but she insisted it be you who takes care of it. Could you do that?"

Officer Dan swallowed hard. I could tell by the bulging vein in his forehead that he was working hard to restrain his anger. "You bet I will. I'll make sure that bastard is put away for doing this."

"There's more," I said.

Officer Dan drank from his soda. His nostrils were moving when he breathed.

"I think...Well, I don't know for sure, but I have a feeling he might have a little more on his conscience than beating up Sophia."

"What? You mean like he has done this to more women?"

"Not just that. I think that maybe...I can't prove anything, but maybe he might have killed the others as well. You know, Mrs. Hein-richsen, Irene Justesen, the Pastor, and even my grandmother."

"Interesting theory. Why do you say that?" Officer Dan asked.

"It's gonna sound strange, but...well, first of all, he's a psychopath, right?"

Officer Dan nodded. "To do that kind of a thing to a girl like Sophia, he must be."

"Okay, so he's capable of hurting people and maybe even killing, that was my first clue. Second, he served us something really weird for dinner the other night."

"Oh, like what?"

"Hearts and liver."

Officer Dan spurted out his soda in the air. "You're kidding me right?"

"No, I'm not. Just like what the killer removes from the victims. Except for the lungs, that is."

"Exactly," Officer Dan said. "Wait. How do you even know about that? It hasn't been in any papers or anything."

I blushed. I had said too much. It was very illegal what I did, hacking my way into the police files, and I could go to jail for doing so. "Uh..."

Suddenly, our conversation was interrupted by a loud scream coming from Victor in the living room. I jumped up and ran in there.

Victor was standing with his big dirty shoes on the couch and shrieking.

"Victor!" I yelled. "What are you doing?"

"Spiders, spiders!" he yelled.

"That again. I'm so sorry, Officer Dan, but my son has been afraid of spiders ever since we moved here, and he keeps thinking he sees them everywhere."

Officer Dan nodded. "Well, we do have a lot of spiders on this island. Some people just don't like them."

"I'm sorry," I said. "I'll get him home. There has been a little too much change lately for him to handle."

"No worries," Officer Dan said. "I'll take care of that thing we discussed. Be sure of that. I'll be at the station later today, and then I'll visit Sophia to take her statement. I'll bring Stephan Olsen in as soon as possible. We'll have him locked up soon enough. I've got it. Don't worry."

I tried to grab Victor, but he started screaming louder as my hand touched his arm. "Victor!" I said angrily. "This is not the time for this. We have to get home before the snow covers all the streets and it gets too slippery."

But Victor kept screaming and pulling his hand away.

"Wait a minute," Officer Dan said and removed my hand from Victor's arm. "Something is hurting him." He turned to look at Victor, then spoke to him gently. "Is your arm hurting?"

Victor stopped screaming and sniffled. Then he nodded. "Okay, Victor. Can you pull up your sleeve and let us look at your arm? We won't touch it if you don't want us to, all right?"

Victor nodded again, then carefully pulled up the sleeve of his jacket and shirt. Red marks appeared on his skin.

"Oh, I forgot," I said and held a hand in front of my mouth. "The insect bites. But I thought they were gone now? They seem all red and inflamed again."

Officer Dan looked at them closer. "They can get like that if he keeps scratching them. This doesn't look good at all. You know what those are? Those are spider bites."

"Spider bites?"

Officer Dan nodded. "Yup. I'd recognize these anywhere. Used to get them a lot as a kid. All the time, actually. Where I grew up, spiders were everywhere."

"So, that's why he's so scared of spiders?"

"Has he been playing in your yard a lot?"

"Yes. Yes, he has."

"Well, that's it then. The yard behind your house is packed with spiders. The *Atypus Affinis* or the Northern Tarantula, as it's also called. They have a quite strong bite. It's not dangerous, but it can hurt for quite a while."

"Wow. I guess that's it, huh, Vic? Good to know what it is, thank you, Officer Dan. For all your help."

"It was my pleasure," he said.

I walked towards the door with Victor right behind me. As I grabbed the handle, it suddenly dawned on me. I turned and looked at him. My body started shaking as I recognized his eyes.

"You're him, aren't you? You're that boy. How else would you know that my grandmother's yard is filled with these spiders? You're the boy from the bunker underground, aren't you? You had a spider on your face. That's how you got bitten all the time as a kid. You played with them down there, didn't you? It's not a common spider on this island, or else Doctor Williamsen would have seen that kind of bite before. But he hadn't. It's only in that yard, isn't it?"

Officer Dan took in a deep breath. "You got me there."

Then he sprang for the door and locked it.

52

2012

"What's going on here, Dan?" I said, my voice slightly shaking. "Why did you lock the door?"

Officer Dan shook his head. "I'm sorry. I'm afraid I can't let you leave."

"What are you talking about?" I felt Victor's hand in mine. It could only mean he was afraid. Just like I was beginning to be. I hadn't yet put all the pieces together, but I was beginning to.

"It was you?" I asked.

Officer Dan walked closer to us. Victor was climbing behind me, whimpering in fear. I backed up slowly. "You killed my grandmother? You killed all those people?"

Officer Dan didn't react. He kept walking closer to us.

"She kept you in that bunker in the yard, didn't she? Was that why she had to die? Was that why you killed her? She was the first, she was number five. Why did you kill the rest of them? Were they in on it?" I stared into his eyes as I spoke, and all the while I was trying to grab something, anything I could find on my way backwards to be able to throw at him or hit him with. I walked into a lamp and almost tipped it over. Then I grabbed it and threw it at him. He grabbed it mid-air and put it down with a grin. "You're no match for me," he said. "I dealt with guys twice my size growing up at the orphanage after you let me out."

"So, you do remember me?" I asked desperately, searching for something to defend myself with.

"Of course I do. And I really hate to have to kill you, since you actually saved my life. You're the reason I am alive."

"What were you even doing in that bunker? Why were you locked up down there?"

Victor was clenching my hand hard now. Officer Dan stopped. Then he walked sideways to the fireplace and grabbed a fire poker. I gasped when he raised it in the air. I gulped when, all of a sudden, the last pieces fell into place.

"You were born down there, weren't you? Your mom is Irene Justesen's daughter, who disappeared when she was sixteen. She was pregnant. Someone must have locked her in that bunker, where she gave birth to her baby, right?" I gasped and held a hand to my mouth. "My grandmother? My grandmother did that to her?"

Officer Dan nodded.

"But why? Why would she do that to you and your mother? I don't understand." Thoughts were rolling through my head now, and I had a hard time keeping them in control. "You were really born in that shelter?"

"Born and spent the first seven years of my life down there. Until you came along and let me out."

I almost fell backwards, thinking about the cruelty of this truth. The gruesomeness displayed by my own grandmother. Officer Dan came closer, and now he swung the fire poker against me. I screamed and ducked, while pushing Victor to the ground so he wouldn't be hit. Officer Dan grunted, then lifted the poker again. I was afraid now, my heart pounding rapidly. I needed to keep talking to try and extend my time, time to figure out what to do. I needed to keep talking.

"So, tell me, what did you do with the organs you cut out of your victims?" I asked, slightly afraid of the answer. I had an idea what he might have been doing with them, but I really didn't like to think of it.

"The same thing I'm gonna do with yours when I'm done with you." Officer Dan smiled widely, then swung the fire poker at me again. I ducked once again, but he managed to hit me on my shoulder. It hurt like crazy. I screamed. The poker bounced off my shoulder and poked a hole in the wall.

"Mommy? Are you okay?" Victor asked when he saw me throw myself to the ground, screaming and holding a hand to my bleeding shoulder.

"I'm okay, Victor. It just hurts like hell." I looked up and saw Officer Dan standing, bent over me with the fire poker lifted in the air. Victor shrieked.

"You ate them, you filthy pig. Didn't you? You ate them."

Officer Dan laughed. "You could say I developed a taste for human flesh while I was in the bunker."

I stared at him while trying to get up. Officer Dan planted his big boot on my stomach and pressed me down.

"Your mother," I moaned. "She wasn't there when I opened the door. You ate her, too, didn't you?"

Officer Dan laughed again, then swung the fire poker towards my head. I screamed as I watched the poker come closer, when suddenly out of the corner of my eye I saw Victor pick up a golden Buddha statue and throw it at Officer Dan's head. I closed my eyes, hoping the Buddha would be faster than the poker, and as I heard a thud and opened them again, I watched the poker come down from the air and saw Officer Dan knock his head against the tiles.

I jumped up and grabbed Victor by the hand. He was staring open-mouthed at Officer Dan, who lay on the floor with blood running from his forehead. I think Victor was in some state of shock. Quickly, I pulled him away, but as I did, I sensed resistance. I turned and saw that Officer Dan had grabbed Victor's leg and was also pulling him. Victor looked at me for help.

"Mommy?"

"Let go of him, you bastard!" I cried.

But Officer Dan was quickly back up on his feet, and now he managed to grab Victor and lift him up and out of my hands.

"Put him down. He has done nothing to you. He has nothing to do with all this."

Officer Dan grinned while Victor tried to kick and hit him to get loose, but the older man outweighed him. I stormed against the officer and managed to push him backwards onto the couch, where he hit the back hard. The motion caused Victor to fall to the ground, but Officer Dan was back up again quickly. The policeman leaned forward and grabbed Victor, then the man lifted his leg and kicked me in my stomach; I flew backwards into the wall, bashing my head and neck badly. I slid to the ground, hearing Victor yelling for me.

"Mommy!! Mommy!!!"

"Mommy's coming," I mumbled, but somehow I couldn't get my eyes to open. They felt so heavy and everything inside of my head was spinning so fast. I realized I was losing grip on what was real and what was a dream as I dozed off and suddenly found myself floating in a sea of nothing but darkness and stars.

"Mommy's coming now."

But I didn't. I couldn't.

53

2012

My head hurt insanely when I woke up. I tried to move, but couldn't. I looked around me and realized I was shackled to a radiator with a pair of police handcuffs.

"What a cliché," I said, and tried in vain to move my hands. I scanned the room I was in. It seemed to be his bedroom. I realized there was someone on the bed. I saw a pair of sneakers and jeans and realized it was Victor.

"Victor?"

"Mom?" he said and lifted his head. His hands were tied to the end of the bed.

"Are you all right, Victor? Has he hurt you?"

Victor shook his head fast. "No. No, he hasn't, but I'm scared, Mommy. I'm so scared."

"I understand, buddy. But we need to stay calm now, okay? It's important not to panic. We need to be able to think clearly. Can you help me do that?"

I could tell he was breathing heavily. I tried to smile to calm him down. I didn't know if he could see it. Outside the window, it was still snowing heavily, and I could hear the strong winds squeaking.

The door opened and Officer Dan entered. He was smiling widely. "Oh, you're awake. Good. Just in time."

"Just let us go now, Dan. I understand why you're mad at all these people who hurt you and your mother, I really do, but please just let my son and me go. There is no need for all this."

"Well, why would I do that now? And ruin all the fun?" Dan said and closed the door behind him. "I have so much prepared for us."

"At some point, they will start looking for me."

"Oh, I didn't tell you? I used your phone and called your dad. Told him it was snowing too badly for you to drive home now, and that you and little Victor here would spend the night. I'd sleep on the couch, naturally, once I got back from my nightshift."

"How noble."

"Well, I am a gentleman, after all."

Officer Dan walked towards Victor and sat on the edge of the bed. He stroked his hair a few times and gently touched his cheek. Victor's body froze completely.

"He doesn't like to be touched," I said. "Please get away from him. He doesn't like it when you're that close to him."

But Officer Dan didn't move; he kept looking at my son and touching his face. "Oh, but no one likes it at first, do they, Victor? I didn't either when they came to me at night in the orphanage. But you get used to it eventually. See, it makes you popular among the right people, so when you need something, cigarettes, a pocketknife, they will be able to provide it for you. It's all about using what you've got, what this world offers you. If you get lemons...well, you know. I was forced to eat my dead mother, but it was the only way I could have survived. I was forced to be with these old men night after night at the orphanage, but in the end it was the best for me, since they ended up protecting me when I killed one of the older boys who was harassing me. They stood up for me, they told the police they hadn't seen anything, when in reality they had. It's all about having the right friends in the right places. And you'll enjoy this, too, Victor. I know you will. Because you know it is going to be the last thing you'll ever get to do."

"You leave him alone, you sick, sick bastard!" I pulled and pulled my hands, trying hard to get free. It cut my skin in several places, but I didn't care. "Touch him and I'll make sure to kill you."

Officer Dan kept looking at Victor. Victor wasn't moving. He was whimpering, his body shaking heavily. "Don't you listen to her, Victor. It's all about you and me now. I'll make your death as pleasurable as humanly possible."

Then, Officer Dan unfastened Victor's belt and started pulling down his pants. I was screaming in anger by now, yelling, spitting, but he paid no attention to me. It was as if the angrier I was, the more he enjoyed it.

I watched him pull down Victor's underwear, and then I started crying. "Please, please! Take me instead. I'll do anything! ANYTHING! Just not that. Just don't touch my son!"

Officer Dan glanced at me. At the bedside table next to Victor he had placed two knives. One of them was a scalpel. I had a vague idea what his plan was with my son, and it made me feel sick.

"Don't hurt him. Don't hurt him!"

Officer Dan moved towards Victor's crotch, while glaring at me like my anger and desperation were feeding him, nourishing his cruelty.

"Now, just close your eyes and enjoy this," Officer Dan said to Victor, as he opened his mouth and leaned over Victor's crotch.

54

2012

"NO!!!" I was screaming at the top of my lungs. I whimpered and sobbed hysterically, feeling hopeless, helpless, and abandoned.

Officer Dan suddenly stopped. His body froze and he lifted his head and stared at Victor. It took me a few seconds to realize what was wrong. Victor's body was shaking heavily, and now he started screaming. A high-pitched, bone-piercing scream that I knew all too well.

Victor was having one of his seizures!

"What the hell?" Officer Dan said and moved away. Victor's body was moving in spasms, his upper body looking like a bow above the bed. Officer Dan turned to look at me. "What's wrong with him?"

"He's having a seizure. I told you he doesn't like to be touched. Let me free and I'll help him."

Officer Dan looked at Victor, then back at me.

"Please, let me help him. He might swallow his tongue. At least turn him so he's not on his back. Please?"

"No. No. I can't." I could tell Officer Dan was freaking out now. Then he looked at me with a grin. "Well, I guess I'll just leave him like this. You can watch him die, then. It's not quite what I planned, but it might turn out to be even better."

"No. You have to help him. You can't do this! Why are you so cruel towards my son and me? What have we ever done to you?"

Officer Dan walked closer to me, then bent down towards me. I groaned and tried to kick him, but had no luck.

"You stole my childhood. You had the life I should have had," he said. "Now you have to excuse me. I have somewhere to be. Hope you'll enjoy the show while I'm gone. I can't wait to hear the details on how your son died when I come back. My favorite moment watching someone die is when they take that last breath, do they scream, or do they pass on quietly? It's never quite the same. Each person has his or her own way to go. It's quite fascinating."

"You're sick."

Officer Dan walked towards the door and opened it. He looked at me one last time before he left. "You kids be good," he said and waved, moving all of his fingers.

Then he was gone.

"Victor?" I said. "Victor, are you alright?"

The entire bed was still shaking heavily, while Victor's body was moving in spasms. I was crying in desperation, not knowing what to do. I pulled and pulled on the handcuffs, but it was no use. Victor was making choking noises now.

"Victor. Sweet, poor Victor. I'll help you right away. I just need to figure out how to...how to get out of these handcuffs. For crying out loud!! There has to be a way."

I was yelling the last words when suddenly I realized Victor had become quiet on the bed. The silence was unbearable, and suddenly I wished for any kind of sound coming from up there, even if it was of him choking.

"Victor?" I cried. "Victor?"

No answer.

"VICTOOOR!"

But still nothing. He was lying lifeless on the bed.

Oh, no. Not that. Not that, dear God. Please, please help him, please help me; please don't take him away from me!

I was crying hard now, screaming at the top of my lungs, when suddenly I was interrupted by the sound of glass breaking. Right in front of me on the wooden floors landed a concrete birdbath with a loud crash. Glass shattered all over the floor, and I turned away from it to not get hit in the face.

I heard a thud behind me and turned to see someone jump into the room through the broken window.

"My God! What is going on here?"

I felt a pinch of hope. It was Jack. He turned to look at me.

"Victor," I said, my voice shaking in despair. "Take care of Victor. He's not breathing."

Jack jumped towards the bed and I saw him feel for the pulse on Victor's throat. He looked at me and shook his head.

"NO!" I yelled.

Jack pulled Victor's head backwards and started giving him mouth to mouth, while pressing on his heart. I was screaming, pulling my bloody hands against the handcuffs. Suddenly, I realized the water pipe I was tied to was moving and was about to get loose from the wall. While Jack worked on my lifeless son, I pulled and pulled, and suddenly it came loose. Hot water spurted out into the room, but I was free to move and ran towards Victor. As I hit the bed and started shaking him, screaming his name, he suddenly coughed. Jack turned him to the side and soon after he was breathing again.

"Victor? Victor, my dear boy," I yelled and tried to hug him with my handcuffed hands around his neck.

"Mommy," he said and looked at me. "I think I'd like to go home now."

55

2012

"When you didn't come to see my painting as planned, I was worried," Jack said, as we jumped into the car. He held the door for me, as I was carrying Victor in my arms and the boy refused to let go of me. I had finally gotten rid of the handcuffs, since Jack had found the key on the kitchen table in Officer Dan's house and opened them for me.

I decided to sit with Victor in the back seat. We were breaking the law if I let him sit on my lap all the way, but at that moment, I didn't care. Something urgent had entered my mind. It was something Officer Dan had said before he left me.

You stole my childhood. You had the life I was supposed to have had.

At first, I had thought it was nothing, but the more I thought about it, it made sense.

"So, when I went to your house, your dad told me you were staying at Officer Dan's house, because there was too much snow on the roads for you to be able to get back tonight. As I walked back to my own house, though, I realized the snowplows had been working all afternoon and that most of the roads had been cleared by now.

Especially downtown. So I thought something had to be wrong. I went home anyway, but was feeling very uneasy. I can't explain it...it was like something inside of me told me you weren't all right. I kept thinking about Victor, actually. There was this spider sitting on my sister's arm when I fed her dinner. It reminded me of him, so I thought it wouldn't harm anyone if I went down there to check and make sure everything was all right. As soon as I got close to the house, I heard you screaming. I noticed Officer Dan's car was gone, so I went around the back and saw you two through the window. The rest, you know."

"What can I say? We owe you everything!" I said with tears in my eyes, while kissing my son for the fifteenth time since we entered the car. I didn't care if he didn't like it. Jack was driving slowly through the driving snow that seemed to have gotten worse. "If you hadn't... well, I don't really want to think about it."

Jack looked at me in the rearview mirror. "Me either."

I looked back at him and shaped a "thank you" with my lips. I had noticed he hadn't stuttered all the way in the car, even though he was the one who had talked the most.

I was the first one who saw it. I noticed it first when we drove onto the street. The island's police car was parked in front of my grand-mother's old house. I leaned forward and put my hand on Jack's shoulder. "He's here," I said. My heart was beating rapidly now. Officer Dan was on duty and now he was inside of my house? I felt Victor's body start shaking in my hands.

"Let's go to your place first," I said to Jack.

We turned off the headlights of the car and parked in front of Jack's house. I carried Victor inside and put him on the couch with a blanket over his little body. I kissed his forehead. "What's that man doing in our house?" he asked.

"Don't you worry about him," I said. "Try and get some sleep. You need it. Jack here will keep an eye on you while I go over there."

ITSY, BITSY SPIDER   203

Victor grabbed my shirt and pulled me closer. "Don't go, Mommy. Don't go over there." There was panic in his voice.

"I have to, buddy. Grandpa is over there, so are Maya and all the kids. I need to make sure they're all right."

Victor seemed pensive for a few seconds. Then he looked into my eyes. "Look for the spider," he whispered. "When the spider bites, you make your move."

I looked at him, thinking he was hallucinating, then touched his forehead to make sure he wasn't running a fever. He wasn't.

"Get some sleep," I said, and tucked him in. "It's been an eventful day."

"I have some soup if you're hungry," Jack said.

Victor smiled.

"I think he'd like that, thank you very much," I said, and walked towards the door. As I grabbed the handle, I turned to look one last time at my son, whom I almost lost earlier that same day.

I didn't want to think about it, but I couldn't help but wonder... was I ever going to see him again?

"Here, take this. It's the closest thing I have to a weapon," Jack said, and handed me an old dagger. "It used to be my dad's."

56

2012

I felt strange walking across the street with a dagger in my hand. I ran through the snow, feeling anxious that I might arrive too late. I wasn't surprised to find Officer Dan there. I had figured out somewhere along the way that my dad was supposed to be his last victim. It hurt me so badly to admit it to myself, but it was all very clear right now.

My dad was the father. My dad was Officer Dan's father. My dad was the one who had gotten Irene Justesen's daughter pregnant at only sixteen. Then the church people with my grandmother, Mrs. Heinrichsen, and the pastor, had decided it was too great a scandal, which had to be somehow covered up. Apparently, my dad hadn't wanted to be the father of this child, and so my grandmother had paid Irene Justesen to let them take her daughter away, maybe they didn't even tell her to where. But they had locked her in that bunker, where she gave birth to her baby. Seven years they lived down there before my grandmother went to the hospital with a broken hip and didn't return until it was too late, and the mother had died from hunger. The boy was forced to eat her remains to stay alive, and then he had been released from the bunker when I found the key and opened the door. That was the story, and now Officer Dan was revenging himself and his mother. The only person left was the one meant to be number one.

My dad. The father.

I felt a severe pinch in my stomach at the thought that my dad could have been a part of this insane and very, very cruel act.

But he must have known. How couldn't he?

I avoided the front door and ran around to the back, hoping and praying that I wasn't too late. I peeked in the windows and saw my dad walk towards the fireplace, throw in a log, then turn his head. I breathed in a sigh of relief. He was all right. But, as I looked at whom he was talking to, my blood froze. Right there in the living room, sitting in an armchair was Officer Dan in his full uniform. Probably knocked on the door telling my dad he was on duty, maybe under the pretense that I sent him to make sure they were all okay. Then he asked for a cup of coffee, I thought. Sure enough, I spotted a mug on the table in front of him.

So, he had them all tricked into thinking he was there on a social call. I walked backwards and tried to look through the windows upstairs. I spotted Maya in one of them. I threw a small rock to the window. She didn't react. So I did it again, and this time, she turned to see what it was. I waved and she opened the window.

"Mom? What the heck are you doing down there?"

I shushed her. Then whispered as loud as I could without anyone else hearing me. "Get out of the house. Now."

"I can't hear you, Mom. You really need to speak up!"

I tried slightly louder. "Get out of the house, now!"

"What? Why? I just put the kids to bed. What's going on, Mom? Is this some sort of prank? 'Cause if it is, it's really not that good."

I bowed my head, feeling helpless. When I lifted my eyes again, I was looking straight at Officer Dan. He was staring at me through the living room window. I tilted my head up to Maya. Then I yelled:

"Get out of the house NOW!"

When I looked at the window in the living room again, Officer

Dan was gone. My heart was racing in my chest and I started running towards the door. It was locked. I couldn't see my dad anywhere inside, and suddenly I was afraid Officer Dan had done something to him.

I took the dagger and used the handle to break the window. I removed the glass carefully, then put my hand through and reached the lock on the inside. I turned it and opened the door. As I stepped inside, I heard my daughter's horrifying scream coming from upstairs.

57

2012

I stormed up the stairs and ran towards her bedroom, but found it to be empty. Then I heard her scream again. Now she was pleading.

"Please, don't. Please don't hurt me."

I ran down the hallway towards the sound and opened the door to Victor's bedroom. In there, I saw both my dad and Maya. They were sitting on the bed. I was flooded with relief that they were both still alive.

"Glad you could join us," a voice said.

Officer Dan was sitting in the corner on Victor's chair. In his hand, he was holding his police gun, pointing it at my dad and my daughter. I walked closer and looked at Maya's cheek. It was bruised. He had hit her.

"She's a little feisty one, huh?" Officer Dan said.

"I'm gonna kill you for this!" I said and walked towards him.

"Oh, really? Is that so?" Officer Dan asked and lifted the gun.

I stopped.

"Now, sit down with the rest of your family. Too bad Victor

couldn't be here, huh? Then we would all be gathered together. Big family reunion."

"Where is Victor?" my dad asked with fear. "Did something happen to him?"

"He's fine," I said.

"Well, he was lucky. So were you. I'll find him and kill him later," Officer Dan said. "That's the good part about being the only law enforcement on this island all night long. I have hours and hours to kill people without anyone noticing. It's almost too easy."

"Why are you doing this to us?" my dad asked.

"You remember I told you about that kid in the bunker?"

"How could I forget? You woke me up babbling about it," my dad said.

"Well, that was Officer Dan. He was born in there."

"Born in the old bunker? I don't understand." My dad sounded more confused than ever.

"You will if you think about it," I continued. I looked at Dan. "What was your mother's name, Officer Dan?"

"Astrid," he said. "Astrid Justesen."

My dad froze. He was staring at Officer Dan with wide eyes. "What? ...What? ...What are you talking about?"

"You had a girlfriend named Astrid once, didn't you, Dad? She was Irene Justesen's daughter. She became pregnant when she was sixteen. Do you remember that?"

"Of course I remember," my dad snapped. "It's hardly anything you ever forget. But she disappeared. They told me she had decided to get rid of the child. They told me her mother had taken her to the mainland to get it fixed and then she ran off afterwards and never came back."

"She told me your mother locked her down there," Dan said softly. "Your mother called her one day and asked her to come over for tea to get to know one another better, now that they were going to be family, those were the words she used to lure my mother to the house. When she arrived, your mother asked her to go get a flashlight in the bunker, the big one, because the lights had gone out in the basement and she needed to see down there to get some jam. So, my mother went into the yard and down into the bunker to find the flashlight when the door shut behind her and was locked. For weeks, she thought it was an accident, but later she learned it was your mother's way of getting rid of her. And yours too...apparently. Was it good to get her out of your life? Did it feel good to not have to take responsibility for her or for the baby? Did you ask her to do it? Did you ask your mother to take care of it? My mother thought you did. In the end. Right before she died, she said she used to believe you loved her, but she had stopped believing in it anymore. Now she had realized you were probably a part of it as well. *I wasn't good enough for him*, she kept telling me. *I wasn't good enough.* Do you have any idea how that felt? Do you?"

My dad was in shock. He stared at Officer Dan with tears were rolling across his cheeks. That was when I realized he hadn't been in on any of it. He hadn't known.

"I...I...I didn't know...Do you mean to tell me...Were you both down there all that time?" My dad held both his hands to his face. "I... I can't believe it." He looked at Officer Dan. "So...So...you're my..." his voice was shaking heavily as he spoke... "So, you're my son?"

Officer Dan nodded. My dad was crying heavily now. "Emma... you...you have to believe me. I didn't know about this. I...I loved Astrid. I truly did. But we were young and my mother...well, she was against it. I had nothing to do with it. You always asked what went wrong between her and I. Astrid was what went wrong. She wanted me to stop seeing her from the beginning, and I wouldn't. I loved her, I told her. And when Astrid became pregnant, I told my mom I was going to marry her. I really was. But then they told me she had decided to leave the island, to get rid of the baby. It was her mother who told me those things. She told me I would never see her again. It was the worst time in my life. I lost the one I loved and also the baby. But...But, I'd never imagined...this...that this would happen. I can't believe...I can't believe...I..." My dad suddenly went completely pale.

"Dad, are you all right?" I asked and moved forward. I was hiding the dagger in my sleeve. Officer Dan lifted the gun and pointed it at me. I grabbed my dad just before he fainted. I helped lay him down on the bed.

"I didn't know, Emma. You must believe me," he mumbled.

"I know, Dad. Now I know."

"That's all very nice and all, but..." Officer Dan said. "All this family love is getting a little old. I'm tired of it."

"So, this creepy guy is your brother?" Maya suddenly said. "He's my uncle?"

"I guess so," I answered.

"Stop," Officer Dan yelled. "Stop all this chitchatting. It makes me sick to my stomach. Sit down next to the others before I shoot you."

My dad was moaning when I sat down next to him. I felt Maya's hand on top of mine. I looked up and met her eyes. She looked scared, but still managed to be worried about me. Suddenly, she was all so grown up. I felt the dagger in my sleeve again. I knew I could have a shot at stabbing him in the neck, but I didn't know when the smart time to move would be. It was our only and last chance to make it out alive. But there was also the risk of him shooting my daughter or my dad in the process.

I was breathing heavily, an anxious feeling growing in my stomach. I don't think I'd ever been that scared in my life. I stared at Officer Dan, who seemed to be in some sort of world of his own. Maybe he was just trying to figure out how to kill us and in what order. He rubbed his forehead like he was tired. The gun was resting in his lap. While speculating about when my move should be, I suddenly spotted it. I spotted a spider crawling up Officer Dan's leg. Remembering what Victor had said, I held my breath as it climbed up into his lap and onto his hand, where it stopped. Officer Dan felt it now and looked down. Then he smiled.

"Now, where did you come from, little buddy?" he said, then suddenly let out a loud scream and jumped out of the chair, the gun falling to the floor.

"It bit me, the little shit bit me! " He yelled and trampled on the spider that had fallen on the ground.

When the spider bites, you make your move.

Without thinking twice, I leaped from the bed and buried the dagger in Officer Dan's throat. It must have hit a main artery because the amount of blood that spurted out from him was overwhelming. I was covered in it, and so were the floor and the bed. Maya was screaming when the blood hit her face. I screamed to both her and my dad to *get the hell out of here*, while I watched Officer Dan grab the handle of the dagger with his hand, then turn to look at me as if to say something, before his eyes rolled back in his head and he fell to the ground.

EPILOGUE
NOVEMBER 2012

"I t's too bad he turned out to be a nutcase. I would really have liked to have a son," my dad said and poked me with his elbow.

It was a month later, and we had gone to the cemetery to put fresh flowers on my brother's new grave and on my grandmother's. We had chosen to place the two of them next to one another.

Maya and Victor had both gone back to school, and Sophia was well enough to take care of her own children again. Stephan was caught by the police on the mainland for beating some girl up in a nightclub and was put away. Sophia was looking forward to having a spring baby for once, since all of her other kids were born in the winter.

Luckily, the police had believed our story, crazy as it was. Well, maybe they didn't quite believe everything of it, but at least enough to not get us in trouble.

My dad had left to go back to Copenhagen, but had returned this weekend to visit us again.

"Yeah. I bet you would. And I would have liked to have a brother," I said and kneeled at my grandmother's grave to put down the flowers.

My dad shook his head slowly. "Some strange story, huh?"

"I know. I still wonder why Grandmother left the house to me. I mean, you got all the money, right?"

"Sure did. I have decided to give it to an orphanage in Copenhagen, though. Don't quite feel like I should keep it after all this."

"I know what you mean. But I will keep the house. I like it here. I am still wondering if she gave it to me for a reason, though."

"How so?"

"Well, she must have known that I was the one who let out the boy. Anyone else would have said something or gone to the police. So maybe she wanted me to remember? Maybe she, in her own strange way, was trying to make up for the past? Maybe she hoped I would pursue the story and find my brother?"

My dad nodded. "Strange as it sounds, it sort of makes sense. Maybe the old hag did have a conscience after all?"

"You're thinking she might have regretted it at some point, but by then it was too late?"

"Something like that. I don't know. Guess we won't ever know either, huh?"

"Guess not."

My dad started walking towards the exit. I followed him.

"I have come to a decision, though," he said.

I grabbed his hand and held it tight in mine. "And what's that, might I ask?"

"I don't like being this far away from my loved ones, and since I can't seem to get you to move back, well...then..."

"Really? You'll move here?"

"I'll get a small house somewhere in town, of course. I've already notified the clinic. They seemed to be awfully happy to get rid of me. They can take care of it without me from now on. And I get to be with my family. It's a win-win."

"Promise me you won't live in my house, though."

"Oh, I wouldn't even think about it. Hate that place...remember? Never slept well there. No, I need my own place."

I put my arm around his shoulder.

"Sounds great, Dad. Sounds really great."

As we came closer to the car, I noticed a small spider crawling on my leg. I picked it up in my hand and looked at it. Then I put it down on the ground and decided not to kill it.

I guess I felt like I owed it one.

The End

———

Want to know what happens next?
Get the sequel ***MISS POLLY HAD A DOLLY*** here:
https://readerlinks.com/l/190533

AFTERWORD

Dear Reader,

Thank you for purchasing *Itsy, Bitsy Spider*. I hope you enjoyed it. This is the first book in my series about Emma Frost and her family on the island of Fanoe. You can get the other books in the series by following the links on the next pages.

If you liked *Itsy, Bitsy Spider*, then you might enjoy my other mystery-series, the Rebekka Franck Series. It takes place in Denmark, as well, and begins with the first book *One, Two... He is Coming for You*.

Don't forget to check out my other books if you haven't already read them. Just follow the links below. And don't forget to leave reviews, if you can.

Take care,
Willow

To be the first to hear about new releases and bargains from Willow Rose, sign up below to be on the

VIP List. (I promise not to share your email with anyone else, and I won't clutter your inbox.)

- Tap here to sign up to be on the VIP LIST -

Tired of too many emails? Text the word: "willowrose" to 31996 to sign up to Willow's VIP text List to get a text alert with news about New Releases, Giveaways, Bargains and Free books from Willow.

Follow Willow Rose on BookBub:

Follow Willow on BookBub

Connect with Willow online:
Facebook
Twitter
GoodReads
willow-rose.net
madamewillowrose@gmail.com

ABOUT THE AUTHOR

The Queen of Scream aka Willow Rose is a #1 Amazon Best-selling Author and an Amazon ALL-star Author of more than 80 novels. She writes Mystery, Paranormal, Romance, Suspense, Horror, Supernatural thrillers, and Fantasy.

Willow's books are fast-paced, nail-biting page-turners with twists you won't see coming.

Several of her books have reached the Kindle top 20 of ALL books in the US, UK, and Canada.

She has sold more than four million books all over the world.

Willow lives on Florida's Space Coast with her husband and two daughters. When she is not writing or reading, you will find her surfing and watch the dolphins play in the waves of the Atlantic Ocean.

——

To be the first to hear about new releases and bargains —from Willow Rose—sign up below to be on the VIP List. (I promise not to share your email with anyone else, and I won't clutter your inbox.)

Sign up to be on the VIP LIST here:

http://readerlinks.com/l/415254

Tired of too many emails? Text the word: "willowrose" to 31996 to sign up to Willow's VIP text List to get a text alert with news about New Releases, Giveaways, Bargains and Free books from Willow.

FOLLOW WILLOW ROSE ON BOOKBUB:
https://www.bookbub.com/authors/willow-rose

CONNECT WITH WILLOW ONLINE:
AUTHOR WEBSITE:
Http://www.willow-rose.net
EMAIL:
madamewillowrose@gmail.com
AMAZON AUTHOR PAGE:
https://www.amazon.com/Willow-Rose/e/B004X2WHBQ
FACEBOOK:
https://www.facebook.com/willowredrose/
TWITTER:
https://twitter.com/madamwillowrose
GOODREADS:
http://www.goodreads.com/author/show/
4804769.Willow_Rose

Milton Keynes UK
Ingram Content Group UK Ltd.
UKHW040643090824
446563UK00017B/152